SCOR

A BILLIONAIRE

NOVELLA

max monroe

Scoring Her (Billionaire Bad Boys, #3.5)
Published by Max Monroe LLC © 2016, Max Monroe

ISBN-13: 978-1540499387
ISBN-10: 1540499383

Editing by Silently Correcting Your Grammar
Formatting by Champagne Formats
Cover Design by Perfect Pear Creative

DEDICATION

To The Bookworm Box.
Please enjoy our hip hop poem (paired to "Baby Got Back") even though it sucks.

Oh, my God, Max, look at her books.
There are just *so* many.
This looks like one of those bookstores.
But you know who understands bookstores?
Authors.

We like books and we cannot lie.
Your charitableness we can't deny.
When we walked in with all that paper in our face
We got…a suggestion.

Cheese dip. You should have cheese dip to go with your delicious coffee.
Pretty much everyone loves cheese dip with their books and coffee.
Anyway, keep up the good work, Bookworm Box.

You're amazing.

If you'd like to know more about the Bookworm Box and its charitableness (is this even a word?) please go here:

www.thebookwormbox.com

If you agree that the Bookworm Box should have cheese dip, please keep that to yourself. We don't even really think the Bookworm Box should have cheese dip. We just really like cheese dip, and writing books makes us *hangry* for cheese dip, and well, this is us writing, so yeah, we want cheese dip.

CHAPTER 1

Kline

"Holy shitballs! That slide is motherfluffing tall!" Cassie shouted at an ear-piercing level, officially waking me up for the morning.

Thatch smirked and flashed his signature wink in her direction. "Hold on tight to those glorious tits when you ride down it. Okay, honey? I'd prefer if Atlantis didn't see my wife's nipples." He reached out and wrapped a greedy palm around one of her breasts. "These are mine."

She slapped his hand away and flipped him the bird. "Pretty sure these are currently baby Ace's property."

"We're sharing, honey," Thatch corrected.

Cassie placed a hand to the free hip that little Ace wasn't occupying. "Awww, are you jealous, Daddy? You want Mommy to breastfeed you, too?"

Despite my preference to veer right the fuck off Cass and Thatch's favorite destination of Pervy Lane, I didn't even bother trying to stop the train of crazy, knowing full well my wife would most likely dive in front of it herself in *three…two…one…*

"Oh, for fuck's sake," Georgia muttered and then pointed a finger in Thatch's face. "Do not answer that."

He just laughed, and Cassie smiled like the Cheshire cat.

For some insane reason that probably had something to do with my wife's persuasive good morning smile, naked body, and sex-themed bribery, we were spending the morning with the entire group—party crashers Cassie and Thatch, included—exploring the water park portion of Atlantis in the Bahamas.

It was a Mavericks' team-building trip with a bonus of press exposure and positive marketing. At least, that was how my wife had presented it to my best friend and her boss, Wes Lancaster.

Georgia was a brilliant woman, and as such, had an amazing ability to multitask, but I had a feeling this trip was about thirty percent work and seventy percent all-expenses-paid vacation.

I had absolutely no objection to this. My wife was happy, something she was often, but never often enough in my opinion. Plus, I could see so much of her skin in her little white bikini I thought I might spontaneously combust.

It was a combination I couldn't have cooked up in several business meetings, and I hadn't even had to lift a finger. Yeah, I was a happy guy.

"But seriously, that slide is huge!" Cassie shouted with a hand shielding her eyes from the sun as she looked up at the giant display of a very fake, probably cardboard, ancient Mayan temple.

"Yeah, it's almost as big as your husband," Wes muttered back, much to Winnie's and Thatch's enjoyment. There wasn't much Thatch liked better than being recognized for his size.

Oh, Jesus. Yeah, I heard it right when you did. He's corrupted all of us.

"I'm not going down that thing!" Georgia yelled, planting her feet hip-wide and settling her hands on her hips.

She was so fucking adorable. And the view of her from behind in that little white bikini reminded me all too well of the moment she'd caught my attention in the first place. Hips swaying, unbelievably inappropriate singing, and so much goddamn genuineness I didn't know what to do with it.

God, she had endeared me to my fucking core.

No, she'd said when I'd asked her out. Vehemently. The idea of a date with me had been almost repugnant, like she might throw up right there on my shoes. But luckily, she hadn't done that. No. She had been intrigued, maybe a bit stuck between a rock and a hard place. And fuck, I had been sure if she would agree to just one date, she'd be something.

I had been wrong, though.

Because now I knew she wasn't just something, she was *everything*.

"Come on, Wheorgie," Cassie encouraged. "It'll be like going to Pound Town with Big-dick. A little water pressure on your puss-ay, a quick jaunt through a shark tank, and a swim in the pool on the other side."

"Sharks?" Georgia shrieked, ignoring everything else in her best friend's pitch with an ability none of the rest of us possessed.

Winnie giggled, still new enough to be shocked by Cassie when she opened her mouth, and Wes pulled her close, happy to feel the laughter of the woman he loved roll through him.

All the while, Thatch looked on like he had everything he'd ever wanted, and as their son Ace squirmed in Cassie's arms, I was fairly certain he did.

"You were supposed to be selling it," I muttered through a laugh, remembering her minor—read as major—freak out over a stingray during our honeymoon in Bora Bora. I hoped, if only for the sake of the people around us, that Georgia's ranting didn't attain the same caliber and decibel it had there.

Thatch tapped me on the shoulder before pushing me out of the way and scooping my wife into his arms. "Hold on tight, Georgia girl."

Her surprised yelp made Lexi, standing close at Winnie's side, reach up to cover her ears. "Thatch!" Georgia yelled as his monster legs ate up the hot concrete between us and the stairs to the slide. "Put me down, you ogre!" she kept on, pulling the eyes of several families and wanderers around us. "I said I wasn't doing it, and that's final."

It was all fun and games until it wasn't. My eyes got round as I watched my friend's hand connect with the perfect flesh of my wife's ass.

"Hey!" I snapped as the completely floored words, "Excuse me?" left Georgia's mouth.

"Dude, not cool," Wes chided, and the sound of his new, relationship-involved thinking almost made me smile again.

"Relax," Thatch placated. "I'm a father now."

"So…what?" Winnie asked with a laugh. "You think that means you can spank whomever you want?"

"Absolutely," he responded.

"You can spank me," Cassie offered magnanimously at the same time.

"Thatch." His eyes came to me slowly, and he lifted his hands away from her legs in a show of surrender. "Put her down."

He bent forward instantly, dropping her to her feet in less than a second. When she swayed from the sudden change, every set of hands in our group reached out to steady her. But it was mine that met the warm hum of her skin as my mouth found her ear. "You okay?"

"Why?" she asked. Confused by her words, I had to pull back to look her in the eyes.

"Why are we friends with them?" she clarified adorably, huffing the wild hair out of her face and pulling it into a temporary ponytail with hands at the back of her neck.

Normally, I would have agreed with her, wondered and whined with the best of them. But today, all I could do was smile.

Because for the past few months, having Thatch, Cassie, Wes, and Winnie as our friends had proved invaluable to a man desperate to distract his wife from the one thing that seemed to weigh down her eyes and her heart with every breath she took.

Since before Thatch and Cassie's unexpected conception, my Benny and I had been trying to do the same thing. We had been trying to make a little baby of our own.

And trust me, I'd fully given trying my most valiant effort, but while orgasms seemed to abound, they were the only thing. No babies to fill our house and distract me from Walter and Stan and their moony eyes, and no signs that we'd ever get there.

The more she stressed, the more I did. Georgia was all I would ever need, but the way she wanted a little combination of the two of us burned in me too. I wanted it for me, and I wanted it for her. I wanted it for us.

Thankfully, every time Thatch bought another set of binoculars or Cassie found a new, creative, and sometimes, even painful, way to prank her ogre of a husband, my wife had another reason to smile.

It was unconventional, but we each had unique things to contribute to the group, and Cassie and Thatch, the freaking lunatics, weren't any different.

"Because Thatch makes us money and Cassie does your eyeliner," I finally answered with a smirk.

She narrowed her eyes. I knew exactly what it meant. "No, never again," I responded immediately with a shake of my head. "I tried doing your makeup once, and you saw how that turned out!"

"You just need practice," she argued, and I laughed.

"Maybe you just need to practice on yourself, Benny."

"It's not the same!" she retorted with a stomp of her adorable little foot. "My cat eyes get all out of whack when I close one eye to try to do them."

I raised a confused eyebrow. "What the fuck is a cat eye?"

"Um, excuse me," Wes butted in without actually meaning his words. "Are you sliding or not?"

"Yes," I answered at the same time Georgia said, "No."

"There's a whole seven or eight inches of plexiglass tube between you and the sharks, Benny."

"No," she refused again.

"Okay, well…" Wes muttered. "We're gonna head up without you guys. See you after."

"I'll get pictures on the bridge as you come down!" Cassie offered, shifting Ace to her other arm, kissing Thatch on the lips with a whole fuckload of tongue, and then heading that way.

Georgie, Georgie, Georgie…

"Fun or torture?" I asked with a smile, pulling her toward me with spread hands on her hips.

She rolled her eyes. "Fun. Obviously."

"Pool or ocean?"

Now she was looking at me like I was stupid. "Pool, obviously," I answered myself, and she nodded.

"Live or die?" I asked and bit back my grin.

"Kline! This is the worst you've ever been at this game."

"Just answer it, Benny."

"Live!" she snapped with a smack to my bare chest. I caught her hand and trapped it there.

"Then let's *live*. Have some *fun* in the *pool* with me."

"Kline!"

"Georgie," I replied simply, and she closed her eyes.

"I want to be on the bridge," she whispered, and a lump formed in my throat.

"With a camera and a baby. I *want* it. And I wish I could let it go."

It felt like a white-hot poker lived in my chest.

I wanted to give it to her, and I couldn't. Not for all the effort, all the money, and all the planning I could manage.

But right now, I could give her a distraction.

"I love you."

She smiled a little smile, just barely there, and sank her weight into me. I closed my arms around her.

"I love you too," she murmured, and I inhaled every ounce of her I could.

"Good. Now get that cute little ass up there and take it down the slide."

"Kline!" she yelled.

And finally, with a smile on her face, I silenced her with a kiss.

"We've got a week of vacation, baby. Get ready. We're gonna use up every minute."

CHAPTER 2

Georgia

"Benny." Kline's soft voice pulled me from my thoughts. I glanced up from my place on the bed and realized I was still in my wet bikini and cover-up and probably soaking the comforter and sheets. I'd been so lost in my own head, I hadn't even recognized I'd sat down before changing and drying off.

When my eyes met my husband's concerned gaze, warm and familiar down to the tiny wrinkles at the corners of his eyes, I swallowed past my melancholy and forced a smile on my face. "Yeah, baby?" I asked.

He walked over toward me until his knees bumped mine and then kneeled down before me. He looked up at me in the way that only he could, open and sensitive to my thoughts and madness but stern with his sensibility at the same time—and with so much love—that I felt that emotion again, starting to bubble up from my throat and spill into my eyes.

I blinked several times, trying so hard to be strong. That's what I had been doing since the start of this, since we started this journey of trying to get pregnant. A journey that had proved to be more than difficult, and lately, had started to feel impossible.

Be strong, Georgia. Just. Be. Strong.

His large hands slid up my calves to my knees to my upper thighs, softly caressing the skin beneath his fingertips and urging goose bumps to appear on my skin.

I had to shut my eyes then, wishing the tears away with everything inside of me. I hated that I was so emotional over all of this. Hated. It. I wanted to be strong and hopeful and positive. I didn't want to face this hopeless feeling that seemed to lay deep inside of me and had started to feel relentless in its intensity.

Because honestly, that's how I felt. Fucking hopeless.

"It's okay to cry, baby," he said quietly, and his blue eyes were so tender, whispering promises of unconditional love and support.

I just nodded, but I kept my eyes closed tight. The effort was useless, though; I felt the first of many tears find their exit route at the corners of my eyes. And next thing I knew, it was a steady stream of emotion down my face.

He moved his hands to my cheeks, gripping them gently and swiping the tears away with his thumbs. "Look at me," he whispered.

I shook my head and kept my eyes firmly closed.

"Georgia, baby, look at me."

Hesitantly, one millimeter at a time, I urged my lids open, and when my gaze met his, Kline's face was mere inches from mine.

"You don't have to be strong. It's okay *not* to be okay."

My lip started to tremble of its own accord, but I didn't want to give in. I didn't want to feel *this*. This gnawing, incessant mix of negative emotions that stirred and brewed inside my every breath. There were so many people out there in the world with worse problems than mine. I had a wonderful and loving husband. A healthy life. I literally wanted for nothing.

But when it came to having a child of my own, I wanted for *everything*.

I wanted it so bad it was tearing me apart inside.

We had been trying for what felt like forever. After one positive pregnancy test had given me all of the hope and joy in the world, and then, it had ended up being a false positive, I'd had nothing but negative test after negative test, disappointment after disappointment.

I was slowly starting to lose faith.

"It's okay not to be okay," he repeated. His blue gaze was unwavering, locked tightly with mine. "It's okay not to be strong. It's okay to be sad. But, baby, I want you to remember that no matter what, we will always get through it. No matter what, it will always be me and you, hand in hand, standing side by side and facing every difficulty and challenge together."

His eyes searched mine, and I nodded.

"I mean that, Georgia." He continued to reassure me. "I love you. I will never stop loving you. And if we're meant to have a baby, we will. No matter what outcome we end up with, what our family portrait looks like, I will always love you and I will always be here for you, holding you, supporting you, and being so fucking grateful that you're mine."

My lip trembled again, and more tears flowed down my cheeks. Knowing how hard this talk was for me, but also for him, I tried to inject just a tiny speck of humor. "Can we have a portrait made with Walter and Stan and hang it above the fireplace?"

He smiled and shook his head, knowing I was ultimately just stalling while I took a moment to find my words.

Kline intuitively gave me that time.

I swallowed hard, and eventually, found the strength to admit my biggest fear.

"What if...what if...the fertility doctor doesn't give us the answer we're hoping for? What if I can't get pregnant? What if I can't give you a baby?"

He shook his head slowly and shut his eyes for a brief moment before holding my gaze with his powerful and potent deep blue eyes.

"Georgia, we are a team. You and me, even fucking Stalter, *we are a team*. We will always be a team. And if the fertility doctor tells us a healthy pregnancy isn't possible, then that isn't your fault. It is no one's fault. It's just what's supposed to happen for us. Baby, no baby, we will always be an us."

I looked into his eyes for a long moment, unsure of what to say, the ability of speech seemingly lost.

"Us," he repeated. "No matter what, we will always be an us."

"Even if we can't have a baby?"

He smiled at that, which took me by surprise. I tilted my head to the side in confusion.

"Yes, baby, even if *we* can't have a baby."

After the words left his lips, I understood. I understood the smile during what was an otherwise forlorn and very difficult conversation. It was the first time I had said we instead of me or I. It was the first time I'd looked at my difficulty in getting pregnant as *our* situation versus *my* situation.

It was the first time I wasn't blaming myself.

"I love you," I said through my tears.

He smiled softly and kissed the wetness from my cheeks. "I love you, too, baby."

His lips were on mine seconds later, his tongue softly caressing and his mouth moving with such tenderness and love that if I weren't already seated, it would have brought me to my knees.

"What do you need right now, baby?" he whispered against my lips.

"Make me forget about everything for a little bit. I don't want to think about anything. I just want to feel you."

His lips moved across my jawline to my neck to my collarbone and down the center of my chest. Between one bated breath and the next, his swim trunks were on the floor and my bikini and cover-up were tossed across the room.

He positioned his body over mine and gently moved us so that my back fell against the soft comforter. The feel of his skin against mine urged a moan to spill from my throat, and his lips didn't stop their seduction, placing openmouthed kisses down my belly until they reached the apex of my thighs.

"God, you're so fucking beautiful," he murmured against my skin, and then he was making love to me with his mouth, sucking and licking and making me forget everything but the feel of him giving me pleasure.

I knew I wouldn't last long that way, with Kline's head between my legs, his strong hands gripping my thighs, and his mouth doing all sorts of delicious things that had my eyes falling closed.

A guttural moan left my lips, and it only encouraged him further.

"Yes, baby," he groaned, and I felt the vibrations against my clit.

I was done for after that. My hands gripped his hair, and my hips started moving against his mouth of their own volition, desperately chasing after the orgasm I so badly craved.

"Come for me, Georgia," he whispered between sucks and licks. "Come on my tongue, sweetheart. I *need* to taste it." He slipped a finger inside of me and massaged that oh so perfect spot until it pushed me over the edge.

Stars exploded behind my eyes, and I couldn't stop the incoherent whimpers and moans that left my lips. My thighs tensed and started to shake against his hands as my climax took hold, pulling me into the depths of heavenly hysteria.

He didn't waste any time once the waves of my orgasm began to quell. His body moved over mine, and slowly, so fucking slowly, he started to slide inside of me.

I wrapped my legs around his back and urged him to move faster, but he just smirked and shook his head. "Slow," he whispered and continued the unhurried pace of sliding his cock inside of me what felt like one goddamn centimeter at a time.

"Please, Kline," I begged and wrapped my arms around his neck and pulled him closer. My breaths were hot and desperate in his ear. "Please. Please. Please."

"Can you feel me, baby? Can you feel how hard I am for you?

How fucking badly I need you?"

"Yes," I whimpered.

He pushed his hips forward a little more, and then a little more, until finally, he was seated to the hilt. "God, you feel so fucking good, baby," he moaned, but he didn't move, seemingly content with just being inside of me, filling me, keeping us connected in the most intimate way.

But God, I wanted more.

I *needed* more.

A desperate whimper left my lips, and I could feel his smile against my neck.

"Fast or slow, Benny?"

"Fast and deep and hard," I begged.

"I don't actually recall giving those last two as an option," he teased on a whisper as his devious tongue licked along the sensitive skin of my neck.

"Kline," I whined.

"What, baby?"

"For the love of God, please fuck me."

He chuckled softly into my ear, and then reared back so he was seated on his knees and my spread thighs rested in his large hands. He nodded above me. "Hold on tight to the headboard, Benny."

My head tilted to the side—not so much in confusion but in stimulation overload.

"Hold. On. Tight. To. The. Headboard," he repeated again, and I actually followed his instructions that time, lifting my arms above my head and gripping the heavy wood tightly with my fingers.

He smirked like the devil.

Oh, hell yesss…

His hips punched forward in one hard thrust, and I moaned in response.

"This what you needed, sweetheart?"

"Yes. Yes. Yes."

Question and answer time was over after that. Kline's pace turned fast and deep and methodically unrelenting as he started to really fuck me the way I had been begging for. I was a goner within minutes, shouting my climax so loudly I was certain the people in the water park could hear me.

And he was right behind me, gripping my thighs tightly and pushing himself deep as he came inside of me on a rough, sexy groan. It was the kind of thing that went beyond auditory recognition and became multisensory. All I had to do was think about it, anywhere, anytime, and I could conjure the feel of it as though it had just happened.

Breathless, Kline fell onto the bed beside me and pulled me into his arms. We stayed entangled in each other's arms for a long moment as he ran his fingers through my hair. I even started to drift off to sleep until Kline's soft chuckle filled my ears.

"What are you laughing about?" I asked and rested my chin on his chest as I peeked out of one sleepy eye.

He smirked down at me. "You're a greedy little thing. One day, you might actually be the death of me."

I giggled and rolled my eyes.

"Everyone thinks Georgia is so innocent, but I know different," he said with a secret smile. "She's greedy and a bit dirty and *insanely horny.*"

"Kline!"

He raised an amused eyebrow in disagreement. "I think you'd keep my cock inside of you all day, every day, if it was an actual possibility."

Before I could offer a sassy retort, my phone started ringing and vibrating against the nightstand. I quickly grabbed it and answered before really thinking through why this particular person would be calling me. Since her pregnancy, I had been conditioned to always answer my best friend's calls, no matter the time or place.

"Everything okay, Cass?" I asked.

"Yep," she answered a little too enthusiastically. "The baby just wants to see you."

My brow furrowed in skepticism. "The baby is two months old, Cassie."

"I know," she said with amazement in her voice. "He's crazy smart. I'm pretty sure he said your name. He really, really, really wants to see his Auntie Georgia."

Obviously, I was going to have to un-condition myself from answering *all* of Cassie's calls. And I probably needed to do that sooner rather than later. I would've laid money on the fact that she was literally trying to push her baby off on me for reasons other than sleep.

Before I could question or react to the familiar sound of soft footfalls across the tile of our hotel room, Cassie's voice was far too close and *not* coming from the phone when she asked, "Do you think you could put some clothes on, guys? Sheesh, I've been standing out here for what feels like an eternity while you and Kline were bringing it home."

I glanced up to find my best friend casually leaning against the doorway to our bedroom. Her eyes glittered with amusement as she shamelessly gave my husband a once-over, paying particular attention to his...

"Nice work, Big-dick," she said with a waggle of her brows.

...Yeah, *that*.

"Jesus, Cass!" My cheeks grew hot with embarrassment as I grabbed the sheet from the foot of the bed and tugged it over us.

Her smile grew wider.

"Mind explaining how you got in here?" Kline asked, far too calmly, in my opinion.

She waved him off. "I have my ways."

"Why are you here?" I questioned on a shout and sat up on the bed, clutching the sheet to my chest. "And do I even want to know how long you've been in our hotel room?"

"Probably not," she responded with a shrug. "And Ace wants to know when you're going to spend time with him today like you promised."

"Pretty sure I didn't promise that," I muttered.

"Well…I'm not sure where he got that idea then…"

A humorless laugh left my lips. "He's two months old, Cass! His ideas go about as far as when to cry for your crazy huge nipples, a diaper change, and sleep."

"What time do you want to come up and get him from our room?"

"Huh?" I asked, confusion turning my expression from irate to baffled. I glanced at Kline. "Am I in the same conversation? Is this a fucking dream? What is happening?"

"Think you guys can be ready in about an hour?" Cassie continued on, unfazed.

My eyes met hers again. "Oh my God! You're insane! Get out!"

She forced a frown to her face. "So, you're not coming up to spend time with your godson?"

My eyes damn near bugged out of my head. "I'm a bit under-dressed to have cuddle time with my godson right now, wouldn't you say?"

"He's going to be really disappointed…"

"Oh, for fuck's sake," I groaned. "He's an infant. He can't even wrap his little mind around the emotion disappointment."

"Okay, okay, I get it." She held up both arms and started to back away from the doorway. "I'll let you guys enjoy the orgasm glow for a little bit longer, and I'll text you when Ace is ready for you to come get him. Sound good?" she asked, but she didn't wait for our answer. "He's going to be so excited!" she called over her shoulder, and then a few seconds later, the door clicked shut.

Kline and I sat there in silence for a few bewildered moments until he whispered, "We need new friends."

I nodded. "Yeah. We definitely need new friends."

"You know if we don't go now, we're going to regret it, right?"

"Yeah," I grumbled, moving from the haven of my husband's postcoital cuddle far too soon. "I'm way too aware."

CHAPTER 3

Thatch

Cassie smirked like a horny little devil woman as she sashayed across the master bedroom of our Atlantis hotel room and toward the foot of the bed, all the while her gaze never leaving the very spot where the sheet rested—*more like tented*—above my naked hips.

A man had to be prepared, and when it came to my gorgeous fucking wife, already being naked was the very best kind of preparation.

Her eyes met mine, and she winked. "Pull that sheet a little lower, Daddy."

Oh, fuck yeah. She was breaking out the "Daddy." *This only happens with the good stuff.*

All too eager to please the apple of my eye, the woman of my dreams, my wife, and the mother of my son, I hooked my thumbs under the edge of the fabric and tried to stop my hips from lifting straight to the ceiling. It was bad form to poke her in the eye before she could get her lips wrapped around the ole Supercock.

And yeah, I'm speaking from experience.
I know I'm normally better than that, but my wife is the absolute

epitome of hot, and the first time postpartum was bound to be subject
to a few snags...
Give me a break. It had been six weeks, for fuck's sake.
The last time I went that long without sex was—well, I'm getting too
old to be able to remember that long ago.

"Oh, yeah," I said aloud as a full musical score of "Get Low" by the one and only Lil Jon played victoriously in my head. *Bu duh dum dum dum.* I would keep myself in control, not blind her or cause the need for an eye patch, and this would be amazing.

Hell, I'd bribe whatever fucking god I had to.

Is there a sex god? And does he or she accept IOUs? I was a little too naked to store money anywhere—at least, not comfortably.

Cassie's hips started to sway to my mental music, and the perfect line of her mouth curved up with wicked intent.

There's definitely a sex god.

I fought a shiver as all the things that sexy look meant played in my head. Memories. Fantasies. Combinations of the two and everything I knew I couldn't conjure in my mind no matter how hard I tried.

I had just closed my eyes against the onslaught of hormones that a dancing, nearly naked Cassie produced when a sharp cry pierced the seduction balloon we'd been working so hard to inflate.

We both froze solid, Cassie in a near crouch, one hand grabbing vulgarly at the completely bare space between her legs, a pink-tipped finger poised to make its journey inside.

"Shh," I commanded nearly silently, hoping that little Ace was putting out nothing more than a sleepy false alarm. Several seconds bled into a deceptive spell of calm.

My muscles ached from trying to stay still, and even my face remained stuck in the contorted, completely unromantic grimace of a man who couldn't take a breath for fear his overengorged balls might explode. Seemingly, just as quickly as I started to relax, a second cry rent the air and dashed all of my hopes, dreams, and dirty imaginings in one fell swoop.

"Shit," Cassie whispered as she pushed off the bed and pulled her underwear up to cover all of the things that should never be covered.

"I'll go," I offered, jumping from the bed and shoving my legs and erection into the unforgiving fabric of my still damp board shorts. They'd done nothing more than lay unattended on the floor last night after my late-night swim. My wife was a goddess, taking baby duty for me so I could get in a little exercise. I'd planned to reward her with this very form of enjoyable exercise last night, but the little guy had straight up refused to give in to the Sandman no matter how much Metallica I sang. But he'd finally fallen asleep now…or so we thought. "Me and our boy have to have a talk anyway."

It was time for him to learn one of the foremost rules of manhood, the crux of everything I wanted to instill in a son, and it had to do with a pledge to abstain from cockblocking. He needed to know that a woman had every right to say no, should exercise it freely and often, and that if he ever felt that way, that he didn't want to go forward with a sexual encounter, he should feel confident in his ability to say no too.

But what he shouldn't do, ever, was be the third party, the outsider to a pair of consenting adults hoping desperately to make love or bang or fuck like rabbits or any form of the above, that stopped said activity from happening.

It was the absolute definition of "not cool, bro." And in my humble opinion, no kid was too young to learn such an important lesson.

"Good," Cassie huffed, opening the door to the bedroom and walking out into the living room of our suite with no top. Her feet made an adorably small amount of noise, much to her chagrin, as she stomped her way from there to the bathroom and pulled a puffy robe off of the hook. "You handle the kid."

I smiled at her mock-disdain for our precious son and headed in the direction of his room as she moved toward the main door to the hotel hallway. "And where are you going?" I asked.

"Don't worry about it," she yelled over her shoulder as she made her grand exit into the public hallway, breasts still out in the open as her robe flew out behind her.

I chuckled as I first heard a thud, and then the completely unnecessary apology of a family man—someone else's family man—caught off guard by the luscious, perfect chest of my wife. I didn't think she even paused, but as the door slammed shut, I couldn't be entirely sure.

Still smiling, I padded my way into the dark room of my son and pulled his writhing body from the crib to tuck him against my chest. His eyes were sleepy despite his cries, so I gave him a few minutes of cuddles and bonding before hitting him with the hard stuff.

When his eyes changed from tiny slits to ovals, I knew the time was ripe for some Kelly-style tough love. "What's the deal, dude?"

He didn't answer, something that was interesting considering he was a baby genius. Sure, most kids couldn't cogitate at this point, but mine was different—as expected. He was the descendant of my DNA, after all.

"I get your need for attention," I told him as I sat down on the couch and pulled him away from my body enough that we could look one another in the eye. "I'm a bit of a seeker of it, myself."

He nodded his head in understanding, or as a result of underdeveloped neck muscles, and smiled with a giggle as the edge of my lips curled up.

"Sometimes, it's even appropriate. Anytime you're with your Uncle Kline or your Uncle Wes—"

"A bit of an attention-seeker, huh?" Kline asked from his casual lean in the doorway.

"Jesus," I said with a jolt.

"Mary and Joseph," Georgia added, as she pushed Kline out of the way and pulled my baby from my arms. "You'll learn all about them in church."

"What are you... How long have you been here?"

"Since your wife rudely barged in on us in bed," Georgia said with a grimace-like smile and artificially cheery voice, her face directly in Ace's.

"You cockblocked them?" I asked incredulously.

Oh, there's irony in this.

Cassie waved it off and sank onto the couch beside me, utterly exhausted. "I didn't cockblock them. The first time, I kindly waited outside their bedroom until they finished boning. And the second time, they were already dressed."

"Cass—"

"I'm happy to report his dick *is* big, though."

I started to laugh, and Kline looked down to hide his smile from his nearly apoplectic wife.

"You're so twisted!" Georgia whisper-yelled, reaching up to cover one of Ace's ears. "Stop barging in on us, and stop talking about my husband's P-E-N-I-S."

"Our kid can spell," I offered jovially, and Georgia nearly hit the roof.

"You're so perfect for one another it's despicable!"

"Aw, Wheorgie," Cassie cooed sleepily. "That's so sweet."

"That wasn't a compliment!"

"Really?" Cassie questioned before turning to me. "Sounded like one to me."

I shrugged. "Me too."

"I *supremely* dislike you both."

"Whatever," Cassie murmured, sliding down and curling up with her head on my thigh. "Just watch our kid, and you can *hate* us all you want."

Georgia's eyes narrowed at Cassie's pointed use of the word she'd been so careful to avoid. My eyebrows rose with my effort to school my features into something normal, something neutral, and Kline took it as his cue to step in.

"Come on, Benny. Let's let them sleep or role-play or whatever it is they're looking to do."

"But I'm not done yelling at them!" she whispered.

Kline's eyes flared with enjoyment. "How about you finish when you can *actually* yell? Sound like a good compromise?"

She took a deep breath and wiggled her head back and forth, but it was useless even if she found the ability to yell, Cassie already lay sound asleep on my thigh.

"Shh," I emphasized, and just as I'd planned, I thought Georgia would officially lose it.

Kline shook his head at me and bugged out his eyes. I only felt half bad.

"Come on, baby. Let's go spend time with Ace. I promise," he whispered as he leaned into her ear and inhaled. It was an act of a man in love and one I practiced daily. "I'll make sure you get yours back."

And, *that*. Well, that scared me a little. Kline was entirely too smart for my good—and I didn't think that would ever change.

As they stepped out of the room, Kline waved with a smile and I moved my gaze to the side of my wife's peaceful face.

We were finally, finally alone, and I was more than ready for action.

But my wife was asleep for the first time in two days, and when I looked at the dark circles under her beautiful eyes, I couldn't do anything other than accept my now universal truth.

This was what my wife needed—and I'd do everything I could to give it to her.

CHAPTER 4

Cassie

"Oh, c'mon, Daddy," I whined and straddled Thatch's naked body. I ground my pussy against the Supercock and let out the greedy little moans I knew he loved so much. "Just one more time. Pretty please?"

He threw an arm over his eyes. "You're going to break my dick, honey."

"Oh, don't be so dramatic."

"I'm not being dramatic." He let out a heavy sigh. "I'm being a realist. Me coming again is a physical impossibility at this point."

My husband was being a big old drama queen. The Supercock might still have been wet from our last fantastic bone session, but he was already getting excited between my persistent thighs.

I looked down and grinned, watching with fascination as the head of my favorite appendage slid between where I throbbed and ached for more. "Are you sure about that, Daddy?" The instant the word *Daddy* left my mouth, he got even harder.

"It's just a prop at this point." Thatch groaned in exasperation as I started to grind myself harder against him. "Seriously, honey. I can't come again. I need sleep and food. Lots and lots of both."

His stupid refusal and half-assed explanation only fueled my crazy to come barreling out of the gates like a racehorse after the gunshot goes off.

See, this is the point where most sane women would probably just give up and go eat lunch, but I have never been known for being sane.
Nope. No fucking way.
This is the point where crazy bitches like myself call bullshit on something like this.
I'd make Thatcher come hard and eat his motherfucking words for lunch.

At record-breaking speed, I was lying on my belly between Thatcher's thighs and the Supercock was inside my mouth. I sucked him deep and didn't hold back my enthusiasm and need to taste him.

"Fuck, Cass." A deep, heady moan left his lips, and I knew I had the big, sexy ogre exactly where I wanted him.

I was a woman on a blow job mission, and I didn't waste any time. The tip of my tongue slid up and down his shaft, exploring the texture and feel of him, while I continued to draw him deeper and deeper into my mouth.

"Oh, holy fucking shit," he groaned. "I have no idea what you do with that little tongue of yours but…yeah…holy…hell…don't stop, honey. Jesus, don't stop doing that."

Uh-huh…that's exactly what I thought…

His hips started to punch forward of their own accord, and no more than two minutes later, my husband came hard on a shout.

One hundred and twelve seconds to be exact, but who's counting, right?
Yeah, I definitely was.

I climbed up Thatch's body and rested my chin on his chest. His lungs moved air in and out at a rapid pace until he finally caught his breath. His eyes met mine and he half smirked, shaking his head. He looked equal parts shocked and awed, surprised and fucking blown. Literally and figuratively.

"You're a wickedly amazing woman."

I licked along my bottom lip and then smacked both of my lips together. "And you taste mighty, mighty fine when you *come*."

He chuckled and reached down with both hands and pulled me farther up his body until we were nose-to-nose. "You just can't back down from a challenge, can you, Crazy?"

I grinned. "When you throw down the gauntlet, you can bet your sweet ass I'll always be ready and willing to pick it up."

"You're insane, honey."

"And I'm all yours."

"Mine." He winked. "All fucking *mine*."

"I'd say you're one lucky son of a bitch to get all of this crazy *plus* a fantastic rack wrapped up in one package."

"The *luckiest*," he corrected.

"Awww," I cooed. "Are you sweet on me?"

His answering grin was the size of Texas. "Like you wouldn't fucking believe."

I placed a smacking kiss to his lips and hopped off the bed.

"Hey!" he complained. "Bring those sweet tits back over here!"

"Pussy playtime is over, Thatcher," I called over my shoulder as I headed into the bathroom. "It's time for a shower and some food."

An hour later, we were freshly showered and sitting inside the main dining room of the resort. We savored the alone time and leisurely sipped our coffee as we perused the lunch menu. It was safe to say we were both thankful for the earlier hotel fuck fest and some quiet adult time away from our beautiful baby boy.

Of course, we both adored our little buddy. But sometimes, parents needed a little time away from their kids. It was a fact of life. Even when you loved your little person more than you had ever loved anyone or anything in the entire world, sometimes you just needed a little bit of alone time to keep your sanity.

Yeah, we needed to do this more often.

I made a mental note to utilize our pseudonannies even after we got back to New York. Ace loved playdates with Walter and Stan. Although, I had a feeling Walter wasn't my son's number one fanboy. He tended to shy the fuck away from Ace's hulk-like baby grip on his fur. Walter—read as Satan—was a total pussy through and through, that was for damn sure.

After the waitress took our orders and menus, I curled into my husband's side and enjoyed the ambiance of a bustling Bahamian resort. A young couple strolled through the hall arm in arm and with a gorgeous newlywed glow highlighting their faces. Four tipsy twenty-somethings meandered by with tropical drinks and beers in their hands as they headed toward the casino. And an adorable woman holding the most beautiful baby I had ever laid eyes on grinned up at her besotted husband...

Wait a minute...Oh, fuck...Kleorgie...

I crouched down in my seat and tried like hell to pull my ogre of a husband down with me, but it was useless. Thatch's big, meaty arm only moved enough to spill orange juice out of the glass he held in his hand. "What the fuck, Cass?"

"Nannies alert," I whispered and glanced toward where Georgia and Kline stood in the hall adjacent to the dining room.

Thatch's eyes followed my gaze and immediately went wide when he put the puzzle pieces together. "Shit."

"Yeah."

"You think they saw us?" He crouched down in his seat, which did absolutely nothing. We'd need some serious Houdini, black-magic kind of shit to make a man of my husband's size disappear.

"Not yet." I shook my head. "But if we don't make a plan fast, the cat will be out of the fucking bag."

"Is it bad that I want our nannies to watch Ace for just a little bit longer?" he managed to whisper impressively without moving his mouth. Thatch had officially gone into commando mode and seemingly had been a ventriloquist in a former life. "I mean, should I feel like a shitty parent for wanting just a few more moments of alone time with my wife?"

"If that makes you a shitty parent, then consider us both shitty parents," I whispered out of the corner of my mouth.

"We're on the same page, then?"

"Yep."

"All right," He glanced around the room, and as one of the hostesses guided an older couple toward their table, Thatch snatched the menus out of her unsuspecting hands.

She stopped dead in her tracks, and her eyes went wide in confusion.

"Just need to borrow these for a moment," he explained and nodded his head toward my tits. "She's breastfeeding, and I need to make sure she's getting enough calories."

The hostess looked at my chest, and once realization set in that she was now just staring at some random woman's boobs, her face flushed red. She stumbled awkwardly over her shoes as she tried to extricate herself from the weird situation my husband had just placed her in. Honestly, I had never seen someone rush two elderly people to their seats faster.

I rolled my eyes. "Real smooth, Thatcher."

"Well, I didn't see you coming up with a better plan." He handed me a menu. "Here. Hide behind this until the coast is clear."

I rolled my eyes, but I still followed his instructions and hid behind the laminated food list. "Is this the kind of shit you used while you were stalking me?"

He shrugged. "Maybe a little."

"Jesus. I can't believe I didn't figure it out on my own if these were the kind of stealth tactics you used to hide your presence."

"I was a little more prepared in those situations," he admitted.

"So you were like full on stalking me? You knew my schedule and eating habits and everything?"

"Yep. Pretty much."

"Did you rummage through the trash for my wrappers and food containers and used tampons?"

His face scrunched up in disgust. "I wasn't a homeless person, Cassie. I was stalking you. And you were pregnant. I didn't expect to find tampons."

I sighed dreamily. "Probably the most romantic thing you've ever done."

It really was the most romantic thing anyone had ever done for me. I mean, my husband had loved me and our baby so much that he had literally driven himself to the point of insanity and followed me everywhere just to make sure we were okay. If that wasn't love, I didn't know what the fuck was.

"I know, right?" he agreed. "My love for you has no limits, honey."

I snuck a quick kiss to his lips before peeking above my menu to see if Kleorgie had left the building. I was met with disappointment when my eyes caught sight of Kline's head. "Goddammit, will they ever leave?"

"Next time, I think we need to set our sights on Wes and Win. They'd probably make better nannies."

I sighed. "I know. I tried them first, even demon-dialed Winnie like one thousand times this morning, but she never answered."

My phone pinged with a text notification, and I slyly pulled it out of my purse while staying behind my menu. I read the message and immediately groaned. "Fuck. Now, she's texting me."

Georgia: How's it going? Is it okay if we bring Ace back up to the room?

"Jesus. Our fucking nannies are stage-five clingers," Thatch whispered.

He was right. They were really doing a bang-up job of cockblocking our quiet adult time.

Me: I have the absolute worst headache right now. Mind if I try to sleep this off for a little longer?

"What are you saying to her?"

"I'm lying to her. Telling her I have a headache."

"Good idea," Thatch agreed.

Georgia: Oh, no. Are you okay? Can I bring you anything?

"For fuck's sake," Thatch groaned as he read her response. "Does she ever give up?"

Me: Awww, you're so sweet, but I'll be okay. Just another hour or two of shut-eye and I should be good to go.

Georgia: So, are you going to grab the "shut-eye" before or after you eat?

Me: Definitely before I eat anything. Not sure my stomach could handle food right now.

Georgia: So, you're just going to sleep at the table? Not sure that's a good position for a headache…

Me: Huh?

Georgia: WE CAN SEE YOU ASSHOLES. GO AHEAD AND PUT YOUR MENUS DOWN.

Mayday…Mayday…the eagle has been spotted…

"Jig is up. Kleorgie is hip to our game, T," I announced at a normal volume and set my menu on the table.

Thatch's eyes went wide for a second until I pointed to the screen of my phone. He read the last text, and his shoulders sagged in defeat as he tossed his menu on the table. "Shit."

"Yeah," I agreed. "Shit."

Georgia: Your baby is fine btw.

"Ace is doing good, though."

Thatch smiled. "Have her tell him we love him."

I nodded. "Good idea."

Me: Tell him Mommy and Daddy love him.

Georgia: You're lucky I love my godson so much.

Me: Awww, and I know he loves his Auntie Georgia so much, too.

My eyes met Georgia's, and she flipped me the bird before adjusting Ace on her hip and walking in the opposite direction of the dining room.

"Well, that went better than I thought it would go."

"Yeah…" Thatch nodded and took a sip of coffee. "Can't say I'm disappointed with the outcome."

"Me either," I agreed and then pointed to the dessert section of the menu that now sat on the table. "I think we should go for the Bananas Foster for our after-lunch dessert."

He winked. "Perfect plan, honey."

CHAPTER 5

Wes

"Are you sure Lex is okay with Quinn?" I asked for probably the fourth time. I hadn't questioned it at first, my little girl hanging out with the quarterback of my professional football team at a resort in a foreign country, but Kline's astonishment when I had mentioned it to him upon our arrival went a long way to open my eyes. He didn't get astonished about much, and if he was questioning it, I figured maybe I should be too. I'd just been too distracted this morning to put all of this well-meaning transference together—*good God, Winnie's legs wrap around me nearly twice.*

"And Sean and Mitchell and Melinda and half the other players on the team?" Winnie asked sarcastically. I narrowed my eyes.

Her laugh rang out, rough and, yet, somehow melodic, through the open space of the lobby, and just like that, I wasn't even the slightest bit annoyed with her teasing anymore.

"Yes. I'm fairly certain that Lex will be fine without us."

I pouted a little anyway. Lexi Winslow made me smile, and I liked to spend time with her. My stupid players were hogging all the fun and beating me out by a mile in appeal. Apparently, even little girls didn't mind a little positive attention from a bunch of brutes.

"Aw, don't be sad," Winnie consoled with a far too cheery lilt and a giggle.

"We're the boring parents," I sulked.

"Speak for yourself." Her cheek lifted and jerked with the pop of a wink as she lifted up the hem of her shirt to show me the four-leaf clover tattoo she'd gotten spontaneously—by Thatch, no less. She said something about it bringing us luck.

All I saw was sex appeal.

God, yeah. Sex would make me feel better.

"Maybe we should—"

"Hey, look! It's the people you're having elaborate daydreams about," Winnie said with a gesture toward the lobby café, the grand sweeping movement of her arm meant to force me into the convenient segue in conversation.

I followed her prompt and scanned the room, but it didn't take me long to understand—Thatcher Kelly stood out like a very large sore thumb. One of those double-jointed ones you can't help but stare at.

"More like nightmares," I corrected with faux glumness. Winnie laughed and knocked my body off-balance with the slight weight of her own.

"I personally think it's hilarious that they just showed up here without an invitation. I'll be reliving the breastfeeding encounter for years to come."

I smirked sardonically and shook my head. "You just haven't spent enough time with them yet."

A bark of laughter startled the silence and encouraged a smile to form on my face as she took my hand and pulled me in their direction.

"Where are you going?" I asked suspiciously—I had a feeling I already knew the traumatizing answer.

"Over to talk to them."

I tugged at her hand to slow her down, but she redoubled her efforts and pulled harder. I followed helplessly.

I'd like to tell you that I stopped trying for fear of hurting her, but she's actually just really fucking strong.

Still unwilling to subject myself to unnecessary torture, I tried reasoning with her verbally. "See. This is further evidence that you're still learning. They haven't seen us yet, which means we go in the opposite direction." I hooked a thumb over my shoulder toward the elevators.

"Come on, grumpy Gus," Winnie teased. "I want to go talk to them, which means—"

I sighed as my shoulders sank dramatically in defeat. "We're going to talk to them."

"Ah," she breathed with a smile and a wink. "I guess you've *already* learned."

That I'd do anything to see her smile?

Yeah, I'd learned that quite a while ago.

"All right," I agreed, fake aggravation roughening my voice. "But you're going to owe me for this."

"Oh, I am, huh?"

I nodded with a knowing smirk.

"And what, exactly, is the expected payment?"

I feigned seriousness. "It'll be tough."

"Tough?" she questioned.

"And *hard.*"

"Hard, huh?" she asked, smiling now.

"Yep. Definitely hard. And dirty. You probably won't even want to wear any clothes."

She mocked a grimace. "I seem to have that problem a lot."

"I know. But because I'm so gracious and all, I put up with it."

"Look up magnanimous in the dictionary, and it's your picture right next to it, huh?" she teased, wrapping her arms around my waist and plastering her body to mine.

"Let's go upstairs," I whispered, too turned on to give a flying fuck what we were talking about.

She bit her bottom lip and shook her head, just enough to tell me that I was completely at her mercy—and that we *both* very much knew it.

"It's a no, then?" I questioned.

Her hair swayed as she shook her head, bemused. "It's a no."

"Just for now, though, right?" I asked as I advanced.

She put a warm hand to my chest to halt me. "Stop stalling, Wes."

Smiling, I leaned in and just barely touched my mouth to the corner of her peachy-pink lips. "Okay," I whispered there, inhaling the sweet smell of her skin. "All you have to do is ask, Fred, and it's yours."

"Ask *and* argue briefly," she clarified.

"Of course." I grinned. "That's the fun part."

"Oh, check it out!" Thatch boomed so loud Winnie jumped. I closed my eyes, knowing we'd been spotted.

I glanced toward the dining room where the two crazies were currently eating and then looked back at my wife. "Way to go, baby. It's officially too late to get out now," I whispered into Winnie's ear. She rewarded me with an elbow to the ribs.

"Be nice."

"I'm the epitome of nice," I murmured as she turned from my arms and dragged me toward the table where a beaming Thatcher Kelly and his braless wife sat cozily beside one another.

What? It's literally impossible not to notice.

"Holy hell, I think her nipple may have just pierced my eye," Winnie said in an aside.

See?

As I sputtered and coughed on my own saliva, she slapped my back a couple of times once we stood at their table. It was anyone's guess whether it was in an effort to save me or make it worse.

"Where's your kid, Wesnnie?" Thatch asked immediately, but there was no room for anyone but him and Cassie in their apparently already ongoing conversation.

Cassie scoffed and shook her head.

"Winnes?" Thatch asked with a tilt of his head.

His wife's face scrunched up in disgust. "No. They're both garbage."

"Yeah," Thatch agreed. "Doesn't have the necessary ring to it."

"Um," I butted in. "What are you doing?"

"Trying to give you a celebrity couple name," he said condescendingly—as if I should have known.

"Bennifer, Brangelina, Kleorgie," Cassie supplied helpfully as she smeared an entire tiny container of butter on a triangle of toast. She held it out for Thatch to take a bite, and he grinned like the fucking king of an Atlantis castle.

"Oh," Winnie muttered at my side, and I had to look down to keep myself from laughing at her. She'd brought this on herself.

"So?" Thatch asked between chews of butter and bread.

I raised an eyebrow. "So…*what?*"

"Where's your kid?" he questioned before gulping down an entire glass of orange juice in record-breaking time. It was no mystery why he'd been the champ of keg stands and beer-chugging contests in college. He was a fucking bottomless pit.

"We brought our nanny, Melinda," Winnie interjected with a smile. "Where's the baby?"

Cassie and Thatch's resulting laughter couldn't be described as anything other than snickering.

"What's so funny?" I asked, admittedly curious.

"We brought our nannies, too," Cassie sputtered, and Thatch actually reached up and high-fived her.

As if planted there by God himself, when I looked up and out the window, Georgia and Kline strolled by, baby Ace in tow. I nudged Winnie's shoulder and then gave a jerk of my chin in their direction.

"Kline and Georgia have him?" she accused immediately. "Is that why you called me forty times this morning?"

Cassie scoffed, and Thatch shook his head—amused. By us. *They* were amused by *us*.

"I was hoping you had some extra Preparation H," Cassie answered far too easily. "Hemorrhoids are a bitch after pregnancy. Am I right?"

"I had my baby nearly seven years ago," Winnie said slowly, like she was talking to a child. I was too busy blinking at the same languid speed to say anything.

"Back away slowly," I urged, pulling her at the elbow. "Retreat, retreat," I added, knowing full well we had to get out of their web of crazy before there was no escape. If we didn't get the fuck out now, we'd end up stumbling around like zombies from *The Walking Dead*— lost, brainless, and not a goddamn clue how the hell we'd gotten to that state.

It was literally a life-or-death situation.

Winnie followed without question, and when we broke the initial barrier of the first ten feet, both of us started to run.

I could hear Thatch laughing from behind us and another smack of their hands.

"Lightweights," he commented.

"Totally," Cassie agreed.

CHAPTER 6

Winnie

"High five, Lexi Lou!" Quinn Bailey held his hand above his head and far too high for my daughter even to attempt to reach. She giggled in response and looked up at his large palm in determination.

"Come on! High five, Lex!" he encouraged in his signature Southern twang.

She glanced over her shoulder at Wes, who stood right behind her, and then back at Quinn's hand that was still raised toward the ceiling.

I could already see the little wheels of her calculating and methodical mind turning.

She grinned at Quinn and then turned on her little feet toward Wes. She crooked her index finger for him to move closer, and he did so willingly and without a second thought. Lexi stood on her tiptoes and whispered into Wes's ear.

He chuckled softly and winked. "Good idea, sweetie," he whispered back.

Seconds later, Wes lifted her up, and she had no issues smacking her palm against Quinn's, her face etched with pride and victory the entire time.

"Hey! That feels like cheating, little lady."

"Nuh-uh," she answered and wrapped her arms around Wes's neck and made herself cozy in his arms. "You cheated, Quinn. You made it a physical impossibility for me to achieve the high five. You're seventy-eight inches tall, and I'm only forty-two inches tall. And with your hand raised, it gave you additional height."

Bailey smirked at Wes. "I guess I can't argue with that, huh?"

"Nope. I'd say she's got a point."

"That was deplorable, Quinn," I teased. "Trying to win by cheating. You should be ashamed of yourself."

"Deplorable!" Lexi giggled.

His Southern grin just grew wider. "Give me three adjectives for deplorable, Lex."

She rolled her eyes as if he had just asked her something elementary like what was one plus one. "Awful, appalling, disgraceful."

"All right, little lady, give me a hug and we'll call it even." He held out both arms, and she willingly jumped into them. Her tiny arms wrapped around his neck and squeezed him tight. He happily returned the hug and then set her back on her feet.

"What are you up to now, Bailey?" Wes asked.

He shrugged in response. "Well…I guess I should probably try to get ready for the pageant rehearsal."

"So…you're going to the bar to drink a few beers and eat some tacos?" I questioned knowingly.

He flashed a wide-toothed grin. "Something like that."

"Mommy! Mommy!" Lexi bounced up and down on her tiptoes in front of me, demanding my attention. "Can I have my iPad? Pretty please? I'll go sit there and just play a game," she begged and pointed toward a line of benches on the other side of the hallway.

"Stay on the benches, okay?"

She nodded enthusiastically. "I promise I'll stay right there."

I pulled her iPad out of my purse and handed it to her, and she skipped across the tile hallway toward the benches.

Once Lex was safely seated at a bench and engrossed in her iPad, I moved my gaze back to the guys and patted Quinn on the shoulder. "Thanks again for hanging with Lex today."

He waved me off. "Anytime you need a babysitter, let me know. Hanging out with that kid makes me smarter. Next time, I'll probably try to get her to memorize plays with me."

Wes and I both laughed at that.

"You know, the sad thing is, she probably knows more Mavericks plays than I do, and I'm the quarterback."

Wes nodded. "Considering she knows more about the players, the team, and the organization than I do, it's safe to say she probably knows your plays better than you. Hell, she congratulated me on the thirteen percent increase in third-quarter revenue last week. She knew about the Mavericks' financial achievements before I did."

Quinn laughed and slid his hands into the pockets of his khaki linen pants. "I'm not surprised. I just spent three hours looking at and feeding sea turtles with her, and she knew more about those little fuckers than the goddamn marine biologist giving the educational lecture to the crowd."

His gaze moved across the room to where Lexi sat, and he smiled softly in my daughter's direction before moving his gaze to mine. "She's special, Dr. Double U. A true gem and a breath of fresh air. I just know, one day, she'll surprise us all with the amazing things she'll accomplish."

His kind words filled my heart. "Thank you, Quinn."

"All right, well, I'm off to 'prepare' for the pageant rehearsal now."

"Order the nachos," I suggested. "They're really fucking good."

He chuckled softly. "It's a done deal, pretty lady."

"And keep your eyes off the contestants," Wes chimed in.

"Yeah, that won't be a problem. I like women, not girls. *Women. Adults.* Legal, consenting age."

Wes grinned. "I like where your head's at. Pass that gem of wisdom along to the rest of the team, would you?"

"You got it," Quinn agreed and then headed toward the Lagoon Bar & Grill, where sharks and fish swam in the shallow waters around the circular perimeter. It was also known to be a prime location for a visit by one of the many wandering kittens at the resort.

I did my research before we ever left the ground in New York. I haven't been on a tropical vacation in nearly ten years. I plan to soak every fucking ounce of it dry.

Wes wrapped his arm around my shoulder and tucked me into his side. "What do you think?"

I looked up into his loving gaze. "I think Bailey is full of shit, but I like that he's being so valiant in his efforts to avoid acknowledging the smoking hot and far too young beauty contestants."

Wes grimaced. "You think it's too late to order a shitload of shock collars before the pageant?"

I giggled. "Yeah. I think you've not only run out of time, but it might not be worth the legal ramifications you'd face for it. I appreciate the creativity, though."

He pulled me tight to his chest, and both hands migrated down my back until his large palms gripped my ass. He stared down at me with a mischievous smirk as he discreetly squeezed each cheek a few times. "I can definitely appreciate your creativity, Fred."

"Is that so?"

He nodded. "Uh-huh."

"And what creativity are you talking about, exactly?"

"You want examples?"

I nodded.

"I really enjoyed that thing you did with your tongue in the shower."

I rolled my eyes.

"And the way you woke me up this morning. That was real fucking creative."

"I'm noticing a theme here…"

He waggled his brows, and his heated, carnal gaze started to turn me the fuck on.

I pressed a hand to his chest. "I think we need to end this conversation before it goes any further."

He glanced down at the crotch of his pants that was definitely looking more prominent than it should. "I think you're probably right." He chuckled and adjusted himself before things become real apparent. "Rain check?"

"Definitely."

Taking my hand in his, he led me across the hall to the benches where Lex sat. Her little eyes focused on her iPad as she tapped her fingers across the screen.

"All right, Lex!" Wes cheered loud enough to draw the attention of a few hotel guests in our direction, but it didn't faze him. "Are you ready to have some fun?"

Her eyes grew big and excited.

"Are you ready to go look at some fishies?"

She nodded, enthusiastic and childlike. "Can we go to Predator Lagoon?"

"Yep."

"Wooooohoooo!" She hopped up from the bench, and instantly, the iPad was long forgotten as she handed it off to me and ran straight into Wes's opened arms. He lifted her up with ease and spun her around a few times as I turned her iPad off and slid it into my purse.

"Come on, Mommy!" she shouted toward me. "Let's go look at one of the resort's fourteen lagoons! Altogether, they hold over eight million gallons of salt water and more than fifty thousand aquatic animals representing over two hundred and fifty marine species!"

God, she was the cutest and easily could have been one of Atlantis's employees with the vast knowledge she possessed about the resort. From the second Wes and I had told her about the trip, she'd ensconced herself in her normal routine of soaking up every little bit of knowledge about the Bahamian destination that her little genius brain could hold.

I followed their lead and watched from behind as Wes carried her in the direction of the exhibit my daughter was so excited to see. Her little lips were moving a mile a minute and most likely filling his ears with random tidbits of information about the marine life and their habitats. Her hands were wrapped around his neck tightly, and the most genuine smile etched her pouty pink lips. His soft chuckles and the warmth that highlighted his voice with each of his answering responses were pure music to my ears.

He loved Lexi. He loved everything about her, and whenever I had the precious opportunity of witnessing them spending time together, I always felt overwhelmed with how thankful I was for him. He truly loved my daughter and saw her as his own. He loved her unconditionally, exactly how a father loves his little girl.

Lexi finally had a father. She finally had the male figure in her life who would always support her, always encourage her, always keep her safe, and most importantly, always love her.

I had no doubts about his presence in her life—our lives.

Wes, Lex, and I were a family. We were forever.

Eventually, I swallowed past my little moment of happy, thankful tears and caught up with them. Wes smiled down at me and took my hand in his, and with *our daughter* in his arms and our hands locked tight, we walked in the direction of the lagoon of Lex's choice.

The instant her eyes met the see-through glass, they lit up bright enough to give the sun a run for its money. She hopped out of Wes's arms and pressed her nose to the glass, her curious eyes taking in everything in meticulous detail. The blue sparkle of the water, the saw-like nose of a six-foot-long carpenter shark as it put on a show on the other side of the glass, and the school of fish that flitted away as he moved closer. Each little piece stood out to her, her visually pervasive brain far and away better than the basic function of my own.

Wes wrapped his arm around my shoulders and tucked me into his side, and both of our gazes were more focused on Lexi than the actual marine life swimming gracefully through the water.

Lex pointed to another shark swimming directly in front of her. "Great hammerhead shark, also known as the *Sphyrna mokarran*. The mallet-shaped head of the hammerhead enhances its ability to find prey. They have sensory systems on their heads, and their eyes are located far apart, which actually improves their field of vision. They also have jelly-filled pores called the ampullae of Lorenzini that detect the weak magnetic field produced by fish."

Wes and I looked at one another with amused grins.

"Did you get all of that, Mommy?" he whispered into my ear. "Because I sure as fuck didn't. Our daughter is too goddamn smart."

I simultaneously smiled and swooned at his words.

Our daughter.

I wasn't even sure if he realized he had said it, because he didn't act like he did, but I couldn't deny it only made me love him more—and if that continued to happen, it wouldn't be long before my heart might not fit inside my chest.

"I'm afraid if the bigwigs at Atlantis catch on that she knows more about their resort than any of their employees, she will most likely get offered her current dream job as one of their marine biologists," Wes added with a proud grin, but I was still trying to wrap my mind around his earlier words.

Our daughter.

His eyes searched mine when I didn't offer any kind of response, completely mute and just staring up into his warm gaze.

Eventually, he leaned down and pressed a soft kiss to the corner of my mouth.

"She is my daughter," he whispered into my ear. "*Our* daughter. We're a family—me, you, and Lex. We're a family."

He leaned back and tenderly held my face with both hands. "I love you, and I love Lex, Win. I will always love both of my girls."

"I love you so much," I whispered past the emotion thickening the walls of my throat.

My eyelids fluttered as his lips touched mine in a soft caress, and I sighed and wrapped both arms around his waist and hugged him tightly on reflex. It was natural at this point, ingrained, a perfectly poised response to the elusive pleasure nerve. Every action of his put another block of happiness on top of the pile inside me.

"Baby Ace!" Lexi shouted ecstatically, grabbing our attention just in time to see her run toward Kline and Georgia…and Ace.

"Looks like the nannies are still hard at work," Wes whispered with a smirk.

A soft laugh left my lips. "You think they'll get a break during this trip? Or are they Ace's full-time, around-the-clock nannies?"

"I wish I could say I see a break in their future, but the little man's parents appeared a little too cozy at lunch."

"Do you think they know they're being manipulated into child-care duties?"

Wes looked at Kline and then back at me. "I think one of the nannies knows he's being played, but he's just going along with it because that little baby makes his wife smile."

"The dirty and despicable things men do for the women they love."

Wes slyly slid his hand down my back and pinched my ass. "Remind me to show you later exactly the kinds of dirty and despicable things men do for the women they love."

I giggled. "Promise you'll show me?"

He leaned down, and in a low, deep, and sexy as fuck voice, whispered into my ear, "Looks like it's going to be a real late night for Winnie and her greedy, pretty little cunt."

Fuck, I love this man.

CHAPTER 7

Kline

Football players danced alongside pageant contestants, and all I could do was watch with the knowledge that this had been *my* wife's idea. Harebrained and a little unexpected, especially the whole teenage aspect of the contestants, on the surface, it was a terrible idea. But after Wes's talk with the players upon arrival to the big pageant rehearsal, I'd honestly never seen a group of strong, alpha men so desperate to look *away* from their female counterparts.

Several sets of eyes reached out to the audience and refused to move, and a few others even seemed to be staring at the ceiling. Granted, there was an authentic, mural-like design of the lost city of Atlantis painted there, but I hardly thought that did anything more than give them an actual point of interest to focus on.

No, the sparkling, low-cut tops of each contestant were like beacons, striking out and reflecting off of every available surface in the blazing stage lights. And as inappropriate as it was, it was more as though their breasts looked *at you*, rather than you having to look at them.

I also found it endlessly amusing how many of these fine star athletes seemed to be lacking in rhythm. Sure, Bailey and Sean Phillips

seemed to be following along to each step, twist, and maneuver just
fine, and Mitchell made so much fun of himself that he actually looked
good—kind of like a baby so ugly it was cute—but there were a few
guys really struggling. If it wasn't so much more enjoyable to find it
funny, I might have felt bad for them.

There is no amount of rehearsal that can save these guys...

Professional football players—an athletic position so highly re-
garded and sought after that we made them *millionaires* with just a
year's salary—forced to dance around a resort stage with fifty-one of
the most beautiful teenage girls in the country. Partnered up—and
they couldn't even look at them.

But aside from the logistical details of this trip and its professional implications, I didn't think my wife had ever been smarter.

The sun, fun, our friends and family, and a whole group of rowdy
players just waiting to garner some attention through mindless entertainment was the ultimate mood-lifter.

Georgia glanced over her shoulder briefly, a huge smile on her
face as she worked.

The feel of receiving it hit me right in the chest like her affection
always did, but these days it meant more.

I knew she'd been struggling, watching her best friend carry and
deliver an unplanned, healthy baby—a feat she couldn't manage to
achieve herself with even the most concise strategy.

My phone vibrated in the chest pocket of my suit. With a view of
nothing more than the back of my wife's head, I felt safe to pull it out
and look. When she looked at me, I wanted her to know I was *here*
with her rather than buried in my phone.

As if I'd conjured it with my mind, the name of the fertility clinic
we'd visited just before leaving flashed on the screen. I'd planned to
check the caller and then send them to voice mail without shame,
but sometimes, plans needed to change. With one more glance at my
work-engrossed wife, I stepped out of the auditorium, waited for the
door to thud closed softly, pushed the screen to answer, and put the

phone to my ear.

"Kline Brooks."

"Mr. Brooks, this is Dr. Taunton. I've got some things to go over with you. Is now a good time to chat with you and your wife?"

Things to go over. I glanced over my shoulder at the door to the auditorium and quieted my voice slightly. "She's actually working, but I can relay the message."

And cushion the blow.

Heartsick, I rubbed at the tightness in the center of my chest with the palm of my hand and looked to the swirling pattern on the carpeted floor. Each fiber of fabric followed the lead of the one next to it, like an intricate course of dominoes, but focusing on its mundaneness did nothing to quell the approaching nausea.

God, this feeling was familiar. Disappointment and helplessness all wrapped together and stuffed tightly inside the confines of my chest. All the money in the fucking world, and all I'd been able to deliver for months was heartbreak. Our friends' antics had provided quite a number of fun distractions, but I didn't know how much more I could take.

"Well," Dr. Taunton started and then stopped with a chuckle. "We got the results back from all the tests, including the blood test…"

I closed my eyes tight and braced myself, jaw clenched and back taut. My muscles were so tight, a simple touch would have shattered them. At least, that's what it felt like.

"And your wife is already expecting."

God, how was I going to tell her? Disappoint her again?

*Wait…*what?

Replaying Dr. Taunton's words, I went over each one as carefully as I could manage while experiencing what felt like an aneurysm. I felt like I was in a desperation desert, and the hopeful words were a mental mirage of clean, flowing water.

"I'm sorry. Did you just say—"

He laughed again, interrupting and confirming, "You're going to be parents. Your wife is pregnant. Eleven weeks or so."

I sank immediately to my knees, a completely involuntary movement, and tears threatened at the corners of my eyes. Denim fabric at
my knees destroyed the careful conformation of the carpet, creating
its own little smooshed craters. It didn't take me long to give up the
notion that I should climb back to my feet, and I sank back until my
heels met my ass.

The feeling of unexpected happiness crashing over disappointment and its proponents in a wave was indescribable. I had never,
in my entire thirty-five—fuck, almost thirty-six—years, felt anything
like it.

Today, I wouldn't have to look into the eyes of my wife and wonder whether I'd be able to be enough for her. I knew she was enough for
me, and she did a good job of pretending I was for her, but the course
of our journey toward starting a family of our own had changed her.
Molded her in ways she hadn't been expecting.

"Thank you," I said finally, wrangling my thoughts long enough
to put two simple but entirely too meaningful words together, and Dr.
Taunton laughed again.

"For the first time in a while, I honestly had nothing to do with it.
This was all you, her, and some extremely coincidental timing."

"Thank you," I mouthed again, but this time, I was talking to
God—I had a feeling this had a whole lot to do with him.

CHAPTER 8

Georgia

W^{ell…}
Rehearsal for the pageant was going as planned.

That is, if you considered a half-goatfuck of marketing propor-
tions part of the plan.

Luckily, I *did*.

The stage lights were bright and strong and pretty much unrelenting on the contestants, and their graceless dance partners and my
responsibility—popularly known as the New York Mavericks—were
sweating bullets from the ambient heat. The sequined-covered girls
handled the spotlights with ease, but the tough, burly men missed
dance steps and squinted every goddamn time they faced the audience.

Hell, some of them even covered their eyes with their thick, veiny
forearms.

But I had already known this would be the kind of display our
guys would produce. I had also known it would be the main draw of
intrigue to fill every single seat in the auditorium, and I was certain it
would lead toward future marketing and promotional opportunities
for nearly every guy on the team.

There would be several GIFs, memes, and social media statuses that would go viral because of the comedic genius that was big, muscular, professional football players trying their damnedest to gracefully sway and lilt across the stage. I was certain.

Sure, it might have been a bit evil for me to put the guys in this situation, but I knew it would eventually be worth it in the end. Well, as long as no one got injured or put themselves in a precarious situation with a teenage beauty pageant queen.

Every appendage and phalange on my body was crossed in ritualistic hope that neither of those tragic scenarios occurred. Something of that magnitude would probably have Wes thinking he could spank anyone he wanted too.

God, Thatch is ridiculous.

"Looking good, boys!" An ear-piercing wolf whistle startled me out of my thoughts, and irritation, carefully contained up until this point, boiled over. I knew that familiar, melodic voice.

Speaking of fucking ridiculous, Dean stood beside me, cheering and clapping his hands in a rhythmic, classy way that only a gorgeous gay man decked out in a pristine Prada suit could pull off.

"Holy hell," I muttered. "You scared the shit out of me."

"Sorry, honey," he apologized, but his smirk was anything but apologetic.

I raised a pointed brow. "Liar."

"Ohhhhh, someone is a bit catty today," he teased. "Is it that time of the month, sweet cheeks? Can I get you a pad? Some Midol?"

I rolled my eyes. It always came back to the period. We as women not only had to sweat and cramp and bleed over the rebuilding of our uterus every month, we also had to listen to everyone reference it. I was half tempted to smear my menstrual blood on the skin of whoever's arm as proof the next time they asked me and I was actually on it. "I think it's amazing that you can keep a straight face while mentioning pads and Midol when I know you are silently gagging on the inside."

He grinned but only after settling down following a shiver. "I know, right? A little more practice and I might be able to act like I'm straight and enjoy eating pussy."

I laughed at that. "The only pussy you eat is from that awful little mom-and-pop deli in Chelsea you still frequent."

"Are you saying they're serving the good people of New York cat for lunch?"

I raised both hands. "All I'm saying is that their chicken salad sure as hell isn't being made from actual chickens."

"Gross." He grimaced. "Stop ruining my favorite restaurants for me."

"I'm merely trying to save you from food poisoning. You should be thanking me."

"Actually, *you* should be the one *thanking me*. I saved you from getting some serious wrinkles around your pretty blue eyes with my sexy whistle. You were all frowny and far too serious. And I'm a little bit offended, to be honest. You still haven't said how fucking sexy I'm looking in this suit."

I rolled my eyes in exasperation, but still, I couldn't stop a smile from cresting my lips.

He nudged me with his shoulder. "Aw, there's my favorite smile from my best girl."

"Where have you been, by the way? I haven't seen you since we got off the plane."

I'd tried to convince Kline to let Dean come along to the Bahamas under the pretense of it being an actual business trip for Brooks Media, but he'd done a hell of a job ruining that argument: Leslie. So, I'd rethought my strategy and come at it from a different angle. A very sexual angle with my ass in the air and Kline behind me with his hands all over it.

Dean was the very lucky recipient of an all-expenses-paid vacation from my sexually coerced billionaire husband, and I didn't even feel bad about it. He was a hoot, a stylist, and the best gay friend a girl could have all in one. But since the second his ungrateful ass had stepped off the runway, he'd been missing in action.

"Oh, honey, have I got some stories to tell you," he said with a waggle of his brow. I pulled him toward the row of seats behind us and sank down in the one on the end while he sat beside me. With the way he'd looked when he said the word "stories," I knew it'd be best to hear them sitting down. "I spent two nights on an all-gay cruise ship, and I never even saw the water."

I shook my head as several visuals popped into my mind, and I focused on the facts. "Hold on...you mean to tell me you haven't even been at the resort for the past two days?"

He nodded without shame and did a little shimmy. "That's exactly what I'm telling you. And I don't regret one second of it. Two days on a big-ass *boat* and the only moisture I saw got swallowed."

"Oh, sweet Jesus."

"I haven't been blown like that since New Year's Eve in 2010."

"Who's getting blown?" Winnie asked with a smirk as she sank into the seat on Dean's left.

He bounced in his seat and pretended to twerk before shooting a hand in the air and dropping his head back in pretend orgasm. "Two days straight, honey."

"Yeah, this diva," I said and hooked a thumb in Dean's direction, "spent the last two days on an all-gay cruise ship."

"Well, hot damn." Winnie grinned. "Sounds like you took full advantage of the all-you-can-eat buffet?"

"Oh, girlfriend, I *was* the motherfucking buffet. And those hot boys ate me up like I was their favorite meal."

Winnie and I both laughed out loud at that line. None of it should have come as a surprise, though. Dean had this hot, boy-next-door look to him and knew how to dress—the boy had no shortage of interested male suitors. Or fuck buddies, if I was being blunt about it.

"Well, I'm glad you had fun, even though you left me to fend for myself." I feigned disappointment.

But Dean didn't take the bait. He merely rolled his eyes in my direction.

"Fend for yourself?" he questioned with amusement. "Pretty sure you've probably spent most of your time riding your fuck-hot husband," he said and pointed a perfectly manicured index finger in my direction. "I know how you two lovebirds work. You can't keep your hands off one another."

"Or Georgia and Kline have spent most of their time babysitting Thatch and Cassie's baby," Winnie chimed in helpfully, a tilt of her head and a lift of her eyebrow the perfect picture of the stern mom face. If I was her kid and in trouble, I'd be afraid she was going to fuck me up.

I sighed. "God, they're assholes, but I love my little baby Ace so much I can't say no, even though I know those dicks are really just manipulating me into watching their kid."

Winnie smirked. "Stop answering your phone."

"Tell Thatcher to call me," Dean suggested. "I'll answer my phone anytime that tall drink of water wants me to be his nanny." I laughed and raised a brow. He rolled his eyes. "Strategy. They always sleep with the nanny."

I laughed as his eyes moved back to the stage and a slow, humor-filled smile spread across his lips. "Or the QB Pie," he said and nodded in Quinn Bailey's direction—well, his *ass's* direction. "Tell him to call me, too. I'd answer. Anytime. Day or night. I'd even bottom for him."

"Does Quinn know you nicknamed him QB Pie, Georgie?" Winnie asked with a grin.

I shrugged. "Doubt it."

All three of us watched the big, burly football players attempt to prance alongside their beauty queen partners, and each of us made a valiant effort to keep our laughter under wraps. But by the time the offensive line had taken center stage with some seriously interesting dance moves, Winnie let out a boisterous cackle that broke the giggle dam.

"Please tell me someone is recording this," Dean wheezed out between breathless laughs.

"Oh, don't worry," I answered and pointed up toward the rafters. "I've got three cameramen up there recording every single second of it."

Winnie's eyes went wide in shock. "Oh my God!" she shouted and bumped me with her hip. "You knew this was going to be a spectacle, and that's exactly why you agreed to it, isn't it?"

I couldn't hide my secret smirk.

"You are evil!" she exclaimed on a laugh. "And a fucking genius!"

"Fingers crossed by next week our boys will have their fine, toned, graceless-as-fuck asses on several social media networks and late-night talk show interviews."

She continued to stare at me in amazement. "Man, Georgie. You play the sweet and innocent card so well."

Dean laughed. "Oh, homegirl is all girl next door, but I'll tell ya, when it comes to business and marketing, she is a freak in the streets and knows how to work it on the down low."

"Did you just compare my business tactics to a hooker?"

He nodded. "Sure did, honey."

I laughed. "You're such a bitch."

"Oh, for sure, but so are you," he tossed back. "You're the one who has a team full of professional football players twirling like fucking ballerinas, knowing full well that a few will most likely become comedic entertainment for the country."

I shrugged. "They'll get over it when they see the endorsement checks roll in."

"Amen, sister."

My gaze moved out toward the auditorium, and I watched as Kline walked back into the main seating area. His eyes met mine, and as I took in his handsome face, concern took up residence in my belly. Something was off with my husband's expression, but I couldn't quite put my finger on it.

I tilted my head to the side and mouthed, "Are you okay?"

He mouthed back, "Got a minute?" And his finger pointed toward the corridor behind me. He wanted to talk, *right now*, and I immediately had the feeling it wasn't going to be a happy conversation. Guts have feelings; it wasn't medical, but it *was* fact. And by the way mine clawed and scratched, he was about to tell me something awful.

My heart hit the floor when I realized what day it was and what phone call we were supposed to receive today. *Fertility test results.* And instantly, I knew; I just knew it was the reason Kline had stepped out of the auditorium. He had most likely gotten the phone call from Dr. Taunton.

I wasn't even sure if I had responded to him or told Winnie and Dean where I was going, but somehow, my feet found the will to move. Kline wordlessly followed my lead down the quiet corridor and into a storage room for costumes.

I glanced around the small room, focusing on the minute details of color and texture and each small tear in a piece of destroyed fabric, as Kline closed the door with a quiet click. Maybe this room filled with sequins and costumes and fucking tiaras was probably not the best place to receive dismal news. Or, I hoped, maybe it would be some measure of comfort after the upset.

I didn't have the strength to turn in Kline's direction. Literally all I could manage was a whisper. "We can't get pregnant." My shoulders sagged the second the words left my lips and, suddenly, I had to fight the out-and-out emotional demand to burst into a sob.

His hands rested on my shoulders moments later, and he nuzzled his face into my neck, pressing soft and tender kisses to my skin. "No, baby. That's not what I need to tell you."

Confused, I turned in his direction. "So you didn't get the phone call from Dr. Taunton yet?"

"I did."

My eyes searched his soft blue gaze. "Well, then what did he say? Do I need to do more testing or something?"

He shook his head, a soft smile curling his lips as he kneeled at my feet unexpectedly. His hands lifted up my blouse and pulled down the waistband of my skirt a few inches so he could press his lips to my lower belly.

"Kline?" I started to shake. "What's going on?" I asked, staring down at him with a million questions and zero answers and the scariest assumption I could ever wish to hope for swirling dangerously close to my heart.

"Our little baby is in here, Georgia," he whispered with awe and love and pure amazement in his every syllable. "You're pregnant, sweetheart."

Immediately, I shook my head.

"No," I refused, too fucking scared to get my hopes up.

His tender gaze met mine, and his fingertips dug into the flesh right at the top of my hips. "You're pregnant, Georgia," he repeated his words. "And our baby, *our baby*, is right here, inside your belly, growing and getting bigger and stronger every day."

My nose stung and my eyes flooded, my heart rate tripling. "I'm pregnant?"

"Eleven weeks pregnant with our baby."

"I'm *pregnant*?"

He nodded, a tear dripping from the corner of his eye, and the biggest, happiest smile I had ever seen kissed his mouth.

I started to cry too. It was impossible not to as so many emotions crossed through me at the same time—relief, joy, fear, love, hope, anxiety. The two words I had been so desperate to hear for so long had finally been said, and I couldn't seem to make sense of them. I was excited. I was nervous. I was filled with more love than I thought was possible. I was scared. I was elated. I was worried.

It was too much.

Was I happy? Of course.

But was I a little scared? I was fucking *terrified*. Was the baby okay? Was the baby healthy? Would this pregnancy make it?

Kline stood and pulled me into his arms, instantly quieting the questions and concerns and absolute hysteria filling my head.

"We're going to have a baby?" I whispered into his ear as our tears mixed where skin met skin.

He leaned back and gripped both of my cheeks with his hands. "We're going to have a baby, sweetheart."

"I love you," I whispered past the emotion in my throat.

"I love you too, Georgie," he said against my lips right before he pressed soft and gentle kisses to my mouth.

He wrapped his arms around my body and hugged me so tightly that my feet came off the ground. They had a long way to go if they were going to catch my heart, though.

I was pregnant.

We were pregnant.

Kline and I were finally going to have a baby.

Oh. My. God. Is this real life?

Please let this be real.

Please…Please…Please let this be real.

CHAPTER 9

Thatch

Heads turned as I extended my strut, striding faster and longer than any mortal would be able to keep up with—not anyone under six foot two anyway.

Ace slept soundly against my chest, the rough jar of my steps not even remotely disturbing enough for a little man in desperate need of sleep. His carrier was pretty tight around my shoulders, but I'd cut the straps apart and sewn in extensions so it fit better than before—when it hadn't fit at all.

Okay. I paid someone to do it. I'm crafty, but no matter how hard I tried, I hadn't been able to master a serger. And that's what I needed—a regular sewing machine wasn't tough enough for this job. My boy's safety was at stake.

One trip to the best tailor in Chinatown, and our setup was fit as a fiddle. Cassie bought another one for herself when she found out, though. Said I'd "ruined hers."

If she wasn't so goddamn hot, with big, bountiful tits that didn't quit, a smile that burned in my brain, and eyes that could challenge any man… Well, I'd still love her. Because being ridiculous was her. And it was me. And it was so totally us that even I feared a little what our child, the combination of the very basis of us, would become. Her insanely hot exterior was just the catalyst for my attraction— everything since then was fundamental, chemical, and completely inescapable.

Several women dressed up for either the pageant or dinner with their husbands or boyfriends or girlfriends or whatever swooned and smiled and waved their delicate but seductive hands in my direction. They mouthed "Hi" with innuendo and sexual offers and everything else the sight of a man with a baby evoked deep in the ovaries of a woman right before she exploded.

A happily married man and a father who wanted to be an example of how to treat the woman who was your everything, I turned a blind eye more than once, eventually just looking all the way down to my shoes as I put one foot in front of the other. I had to look up to inspect the path in front of me every once and a while, but by and large, not looking around my surroundings seemed to be the safest plan.

My long legs ate up the distance quickly, and before I knew it, Ace and I were in the same room with something I never thought we would be—the Miss Teen USA pageant.

"Oh, sweet baby Jesus," Wes muttered from right inside the door, back behind the rows and rows of already seated attendees, as he caught sight of me and my boy entering the room as a unit.

We were both decked out in our best attire for the night, the finery of the satiny lapels of our tux jackets shimmering in the twinkling pageant lights.

"Did you swallow Zach Galifianakis?" Kline questioned through a smirk, his arm around his much better half. Wes and Winnie were to their left, backs to the wall, hands linked and looking aggressively in love, and Lexi kneeled behind the rows of seats and looked avidly at the stage. Ah, but it was a good feeling to have the gang all at peak contentment. The group of them was huddled together in their eve-ning wear, but none of them had taken it to quite the suave extent that Ace and I had. Kline and Wes were both in everyday suits—*fucking amateurs.*

"Ace and I are one hundred percent originality," I argued.

Sure, I was sporting a full beard, and Ace and I were protect-ing ourselves from the glare of the lights by wearing our *sunglasses at night*, but having him strapped to my chest was a matter of sheer convenience rather than a nod to the *Hangover* movie empire.

"You are definitely unique," Georgia muttered, and I didn't miss the sarcastic derision in her tone. But I was completely impenetrable by insult and offense, thanks to the sweet, sleeping baby force field in front of me.

"Where's your wife?" Winnie asked, the first to get over me and my styling son and focus on the matter at hand—the one missing member of our group.

"She's getting a massage."

"What?" Georgia shrieked, waking Ace with a start.

"What?" I asked back, after taking a beat to make sure my little man wasn't in the mood to rage. It seemed to me like some parents didn't understand that a tantrum was sometimes necessary—kind of like their Facebook rant or Girls' Night Out tirade—but I wasn't like them. The human kettle needed an outlet for some of that steam; it just had to evolve with age, wisdom, and experience. At least, for me, that was my hope, what I wanted to instill in my child as a parent. Now, as an infant, Ace's need for stress output came with wild tears, and there was no way I was going to get in the way of that. The Kellys—wild was our way. The same went for my wife and her need for a little relax-ation. "She's a new mom. She deserves a little downtime."

"Oh my God. That's so sweet," Winnie murmured as Wes rolled his eyes. Kline looked to the ground as Georgia's body shot straight into fight-mode.

"She hasn't been watching your baby half the time!" Georgia

went on. "I have!"

Did I mention that tantrums just evolve with age?

I covered Ace's ears to shield him from her insensitivity, and he kicked his legs back and caught me in the gut. He didn't like to be out of the know, and I couldn't say I blamed him. Gossip didn't build character, but it sure as hell kept life interesting. As long as it doesn't do any harm, dip your toe in the information pool and do it often, I say.

"So why don't you go get one too?"

I asked what I thought was an obvious question, but by the way Georgia blinked, her face clearing nearly instantly, obvious was one of those things that only existed in the eyes of the beholder. "Well…I hadn't thought of that."

I nodded solemnly in Kline's direction. "It's hard for husbands to be as good as me."

Kline laughed as Georgia reached behind herself and clamped on to Winnie's arm, eyes nearly manic in her demands. "Come on. We're going."

Winnie didn't stand a chance as Georgia's Vulcan claw started to drag her away.

"Wait a second!" Wes complained, and I shook my head. The prick always complained. Winnie paused briefly, but Georgia didn't exactly take to it nicely. Winnie was like a stuffed animal stuck in the stack with the others as the little contraption pulled on it mercilessly.

"You're not going to let them go relax?" I asked in disapproval before whispering in Ace's ear, "Real men hold down the fort, son."

My voice was softer than its usual boom, but that didn't mean it wasn't heard—and that was my intention.

"Give me a break," Wes said with a laugh, scratching at his cheek with a pointed middle finger. "Georgia organized all of this. I'm just trying to avoid any surprises."

She rolled her eyes. "It's all planned and rehearsed. I'm sure everything will be fine."

Oh, man. Those were famous last words if ever I'd heard them. Thank God Ace and I would be here to commentate as things went wrong.

"Do you want me to stay?" Winnie asked sweetly, and I nearly choked. How my asshole of a friend had snagged this one, I'd never know.

"No," I answered for him before he could.

He shook his head at me, but he did it with a smile, looking around my back to Lexi.

"Hey, Lex," he called, and her head turned to look back at us. "Come here for a second, sweetheart."

She jumped up, jogging over to Wes and looking up at him, her little eyes doe-like and trusting. He swept her hair off her shoulder and rubbed a sweet thumb down the side of her cheek. "Your mom is going to go get a massage with Georgia. Are you okay hanging out with me?"

And *that* was why Winnie Winslow was with a man like Wes Lancaster. Goddamn, if I had ovaries, they would have detonated.

Lexi's smile was bright as she nodded yes before turning to her mother. "Even though there are nearly seven hundred skeletal muscles in the body, only around two hundred are widely relevant. Your massage therapist may find clinical importance in more than the layperson, however."

"You hear that?" I asked Ace. "Take it in, boy. That's the kind of woman or man you want to be chasing. Intelligence is key, okay?" I thought about it as Lexi went back to her observation, and Winnie kissed Wes's cheek like he was the best guy in the entire world—which, seeing as that guy was me, was completely false—and then clarified, "Don't expect them all to be at her level, though. Wouldn't want you to build unreasonable expectations."

Wes's face faded back to its normal ugly arrangement as Winnie and Georgia disappeared through the door, and Kline moved closer to me and leaned a shoulder against the wall. "Advising your two-month-old on the ways of the world?"

I shrugged a shoulder. "Never too early to learn."

"Actually, I'm pretty sure it's scientifically impossible for him to retain that information at this point. Ask Lexi."

I laughed. "Yeah, how's that feel?"

Kline squinted in confusion. "What?"

"You used to be the smartest one in the group, no contest, but you're really unimpressive these days."

He looked to Lexi and Wes, huddled together as he kneeled down to her height and listened to her prattle on about the pre-pageant set-up, and then back to me. "Feels meant to be."

Ace cooed and wiggled in my arms, and Kline's words hit a little deeper as a result. "Hell," I admitted. "Maybe you are the smartest one."

He laughed and slapped me on the shoulder before shoving off the wall with his foot as the lights came down. "Looks like it's time to take our seats."

I followed behind him and Wes as we walked down the aisle to our seats and scooted in past the people who had already been there while we shot the shit in the back of the room.

Three men and a beauty pageant. *Sounds like there's movie potential there.*

CHAPTER TEN

Cassie

I lay on my belly with my face resting on the headrest of the massage table, and the relaxing sounds of soft, classical music filled the darkened room as Eduardo's fingers dug into the tired and achy muscles of my neck and shoulders.

I moaned out loud and without shame when he successfully rubbed out a persistent and painful knot below my left shoulder blade.

God, the room was so serenely peaceful, my body had started to feel boneless and my eyes were falling farther and farther closed with each soothing caress of Eduardo's fingertips. I was convinced he had been sent straight from masseuse heaven just for me.

Yeah…this is fluffing bliss…

"Does that feel good, Miss Cassie?" he asked on an extrasoft whisper.

Jesus, even his voice was soothing. I was half tempted to ask Thatcher to buy me Eduardo for Christmas, but I thought better of it when I remembered that I often used massages from my husband as a segue into any sexual act that would lead me straight into a toe-curling orgasm—and that Christmas was still several months away.

Plus, my husband had wicked huge hands that knew all of my secret spots.

Who needed masseuses like Eduardo when you had a huge, sexy, Jolly Green Giant at home to wait on you hand and foot?

I mean, don't get me wrong, Eduardo was talented, but no man could ever match up to Thatcher's skills.

The music switched over to a soft piano solo, and a dreamy, content sigh left my lips.

Yeah, nothing would ruin this perfect moment of peace and quiet and delicious rubbing and caressing for me. Absolutely nothing. Ace was with Thatcher at the ridiculous beauty pageant for the evening, I had no work to do, and for the first time in forever, I was blissfully alone.

All of those things equaled the freedom to get pampered and have zero responsibilities for the time being. *Hallelujah!*

As Eduardo's hands moved down my back, I started to drift off to that glorious place of being not fully asleep, but not fully awake. The place where your mind was silent and your body was content just to be lazy and half comatose. No moving forward or looking back, just being.

"Cassie!" I heard a familiar voice shout from the hallway. I clenched my eyes and tried to move forward into sleep. Apparently, happy present time was over.

"Where are you, Casshead?" the voice called out, turning shrill.

I prayed I was just hearing things, but my prayers were cut short when the door to my massage room flung open with a bang against the wall. By the sound of it, I was guessing someone was going to be owing Mandara Spa some money for damages.

"Here she is!" a far too loud and cheery voice that I normally loved, but currently really fucking disliked, singsonged in the no longer quiet room.

Peacefulness, obliterated.

"What the hell?" I turned onto my back, for once in my life

remembering to keep my tits under wraps, and found Georgia and Winnie, completely ignoring me and motioning for a couple of male staff members to bring two extra massage tables into the room.

Before I knew it, my peaceful, quiet, and perfect slice of heaven was filled with their chatter and Eduardo's confused questions.

"Excuse me? Ladies?" he asked for what was probably the fourth time. They walked all over his quiet authority like it was laughable. "You need an appointment to get a massage."

Winnie pointed toward me. "Oh, don't worry. We're with her."

"No," I refuted. "They're not with me. I don't even know these weird women."

Eduardo looked helpless, glancing back and forth at us, so I turned my eye stinkier. I had a goddamn battle to win.

"Don't be ridiculous," Georgia chimed in. "I'm your nanny, re-member? The one who has been taking care of your adorable baby boy all day long..."

Okay, so she definitely had a point there. Fuck. I dialed back the stink eye slightly.

My best friend's steadfast and determined gaze held mine until I relented and gave up the good fight for alone time for good. "Well, fuck it," I conceded. "Let's make it a goddamn girls' night. Yipee," I muttered with zero enthusiasm.

"All right!" Georgia clapped her hands. "Fantastic! I'm ready!"

Eduardo looked at them and then at me again.

"Mind adding two more to your schedule, Eduardo?" He smiled at the sweet curl in my voice. It was the one I used to get what I want, and it almost never failed.

"No problem," he agreed with a blush, keeping the special voice's record blemish-free. "Whatever you need, Miss Cassie." I winked, and his eyes shot to the door. "I'll give you ladies a minute to get changed and on the tables, and I'll see if anyone else is available to give massages."

An hour and a half later, we were boneless and relaxed and lying comfortably on our backs while Eduardo busied himself with cleaning up the room. Despite Winnie and Georgia's rude interruption into my alone time, the Atlantis spa staff had managed to bring in two extra masseuses and massage all three of us at the same time.

Ninety minutes of full-body caresses and rubdowns had proved relaxing for all of us.

Although, I was starting to wonder if Georgia had fallen asleep. She had become so quiet over the past forty minutes while Winnie and I kept up a steady chatter of random, mindless girl gossip and chitchat.

"This was perfection," Winnie said on a soft sigh. "I really needed this. Thanks for letting us crash your party, Cass."

"Anytime," I responded. "Before you bitches barged in, I was tempted to ask Thatcher to buy me an Eduardo for Christmas."

I heard Eduardo chuckle softly near the sink in the far corner of the room.

"Would you be okay with that, Eduardo?" I asked in amusement. "You want to come hang out in New York with me and my husband and infant son?"

"You probably don't want to agree to that, Eduardo," Winnie teased. "Those two will give you nightmares you can't come back from."

"Kinky kind of nightmares?" he asked with a waggle of his brow, and Winnie and I cackled in response.

"Exactly like that," Win added helpfully.

Eduardo didn't miss a beat. "Well, I do like kinky…"

Win giggled and I grinned, but Georgia was still quiet as a mouse. Normally, she would've been all too willing to join in on this conversation. Or at least attempt to stop the path of the conversation. Something. Anything.

But radio silence? Yeah, my spidey senses were up and wondering what the fuck was up with my best friend. I looked toward her table for an inspection and found her eyes were open and her mouth was clamped shut. I did the opposite, narrowing my eyes and opening my big, fat mouth wide.

It's got to be big to fit Thatcher's whole cock. It ain't called super for nothing.

"Hey, Wheorgie," I called and victoriously won her attention.

Before thinking it through, she turned her head, and her eyes met mine. "What?"

"What's going on? You're awfully quiet."

"Yeah, honey, are you okay?" Winnie asked with concern. "We haven't heard a peep out of you for a while."

She shrugged a shoulder. "I'm fine. Just a little tired."

"You don't look tired," I disagreed. "You look like you're thinking about something."

"I'm not thinking about anything."

"So you were just staring up at the ceiling thinking about nothing in particular?" I pushed further as I searched her gaze relentlessly. Within seconds, the fear practically seeped from her pupils. Only one thing made her pretty blue eyes look like that—hiding something. My best friend had a secret, and I was sure as fuck going to figure it out.

"Yep." She swallowed hard, but she couldn't hide the nerves in her voice. "I wasn't thinking about anything."

"Are you sure?" I sat up and propped a foot on the table.

"Yes."

I quirked a knowing brow. "Positive?"

"Yep."

"Because you look like someone who is lost in thought, and when someone is lost in thought, that generally means that have something very specific on their mind, and they would probably feel so much better if—"

"Kline and I have anal sex!" she cut me off on a shout before I could continue further with my nonsensical ramble.

Winnie's eyes went wide, and I shot up off the table in absolute shock, dropping my sheet to the ground with a soft plop.

"What did you just say?" I questioned, not the least bit concerned that both of my engorged tits were bared for Eduardo's gaze.

He stared at them for a beat too long and then quickly turned his back toward the cabinet hanging on the wall. His fingers fumbled awkwardly with some bottles of massage oil like he thought we'd just assume he was oh so busy with that task of fiddling with the containers of skin lube like an amateur juggler at a child's fair.

Normally, seeing as I could be a bit of a bitch, I would've razzed him a little, but my mind was too busy with the bomb Georgie had just dropped in the room. *Sheesh.* Who would've thought my best friend had weapons of ass destruction in her back pocket? Though, I guess that was less surprising than finding out she had them in the front.

Gnome saying?

"Georgia, what did you just say?" I repeated my question.

Her eyes were bigger than saucers, but she tried to play it off. "Hmm?" she questioned with tight lips and a nervous giggle, proving irrefutably that she was still the world's worst fucking liar.

"Did you just say that you let Big-dick in your back door?"

"Huh?"

I rolled my eyes and met Winnie's mostly shocked, but slightly humor-filled eyes.

"I'm not hearing things, right? Her caboose is officially loose."

Win shook her head.

"My little Wheorgie, longest running virgin in all the land of New York, just admitted to both of us that she has anal sex, right?"

"Yep."

"And she said it in a way that leads us to believe that this isn't a one and done kind of situation. Anal is legit in their sex rotation. It wasn't just me, right? Did you hear those things too?"

Winnie smiled and nodded her head again, laughing so hard she was developing a wheeze.

"That's not what I meant!" Georgia, face flamed in fifty shades of red, finally found the strength to chime in. "I said Kline *wants* to have anal sex."

I laughed at that. "Every man wants to have anal sex. They have goddamn weekly meetings about it like Weight Watchers to see if they've reached their goal. Like a motherfucking weigh-in. But that's *not* what *you* said."

"That's what I meant to say," she asserted as her fingers fidgeted with the white sheet resting over her body, creasing the corners of her eyes in the least fluffing intimidating aggression in the world.

I tilted my head to the side and assessed her nervous expression closely. "What are you hiding? You've got a secret, and you're not telling it. And you just accidentally tossed out that anal sex thing to try to steer me off course, but there's something else, isn't there? What aren't you telling me, Wheorgie?"

"Nothing," she responded defensively. "I don't have any secrets."

She looked at Winnie with a helpless expression. "Tell her I don't have any secrets, Win."

Winnie grimaced. "Sorry, honey, but you look like something is seriously on your mind. Is everything okay?"

"Yes," Georgia answered more confidently. "Everything is okay."

I decided it was time to unleash the crazy, creepy eyes in her direction. They were Georgia's biggest weakness. They freaked her the fuck out and generally made her spill the beans.

"Stop looking at me like that," she demanded and shielded her face. Her blue eyes peeked out through her opened fingers before she quickly closed them tight again. "Seriously, Cass," she whined, "you're freaking me out."

"I'll keep staring at you like this all night if I have to," I announced. "Hell, if I have to do it while I breastfeed Eduardo to get relief from these goddamn watermelons on my chest, I'll fucking do it."

Eduardo sputtered and choked on his own saliva, and that's when I realized he was still in the room, fingers still busy with those stupid massage oil bottles.

"For the love of God, no one is breastfeeding anyone in this room," Winnie chimed in in exasperation.

"Yeah, please don't breastfeed the masseuse, Cass," Georgia added behind her hands. "That would be so weird."

"Well, maybe you should fess up, you little secret keeper."

"I don't have anything to fess up to!"

"*Georgia.*" I tried to get her attention, but she ignored me.

"Fine!" I responded in exasperation. "Come here, Eduardo. I hope you're not lactose intolerant."

He started to step toward my direction, but Winnie was too quick, wrapping the sheet around her body and hopping off the massage table to nippleblock the masseuse.

"Yeah, how about you leave the room, buddy?" she instructed and motioned toward the door with her hand.

Eduardo just nodded his head and solemnly walked toward the door like the most disappointed baby bird in the whole wide world. His cheeks shone bright with embarrassment, but I had to give it to the guy—he had big brass balls in the face of it. Once he left the room, Winnie made sure the door was shut and locked.

"God, you sure know how to make things awkward as fuck," she said on a laugh as she turned back toward the room. "And seriously, your breast milk doesn't have lactose in it, you weirdo."

"I can't believe you were going to breastfeed our masseuse," Georgia added.

I shrugged. "You try carrying around these fluffing gallon milk jugs on your chest and let me know how it goes. Plus, he looked hungry."

Winnie burst into laughter. "Yeah, pretty sure his hunger had nothing to do with his stomach."

"Are you going to tell me what's going on, G?"

Her eyes met mine. "I can't tell you right now. But I will. Soon. I promise."

"It's that big of a secret?"

She nodded.

"Shit, Wheorgie," I said with a grimace. "I didn't know it was that kind of secret. I just thought it was something equally random and amazing like the anal sex thing."

She groaned. "I can't believe I admitted that out loud."

"I can't believe you let Big-dick's monster cock inside your ass."

Her cheeks flushed red with embarrassment.

My jaw practically hit the floor. "Oh my God, you totally love it. You love to get fucked in the ass."

She wrapped her sheet around her body and proceeded to slide off the massage table. "Yeah, okay, I'm done with this conversation."

But before she could start to get dressed, I jumped off my table and wrapped both arms around her body in a tight hug. "I can't believe you're a little ass pirate. I am so fucking proud of you. Collecting all that fucking booty like a pro."

She groaned and shook her head, but I didn't care, I wasn't done with this lovefest.

"And I want you to know that I'm here for you no matter what, okay?"

"Awww, you guys," Winnie chimed in, and the next thing I knew, her arms were wrapped around both of us. "I'm here for you too, Georgia. No matter what."

"Thank you, guys." She groaned and shook in our arms before admitting, "I love you both so much."

"Awww, we love you too," I cooed.

We stayed locked in our little half-naked hug for a long moment, and then I felt that pins and needles sensation of my milk letting down. "Uh-oh," I muttered.

"Uh-oh?" Georgia asked, but the second she started to feel my breast milk seep onto her skin, she jumped away from me like my mammary glands had shot acid at her. "Oh, for fuck's sake! Did you just spray me with your breast milk?"

Winnie stepped back with an amused grin, and we all just stood there, clad in only our underwear with the massage table sheets resting at our feet.

My breasts decided it was the perfect time to just let it all flow, and I couldn't stop the milk from squirting out if I tried.

"Are you kidding me right now?" Georgia asked as she watched my nipples do their best impression of a geyser.

Winnie just giggled.

"Do they always do that?" Georgia's nose scrunched up.

I shrugged. "Not always. Only when they're just too full to keep the milk on lockdown."

"Jesus," Winnie muttered. "I'm pretty sure you could feed an entire third world country with your milk supply."

"Now you see why I wasn't opposed to letting Eduardo latch on to the teet and have a taste. My tits were hurting like a motherfucker." I leaned my head back and closed my eyes as I savored the sweet relief of the rock-hard fullness leaving my boobs.

I couldn't stop a moan from leaving my lips.

Yeah. Sometimes it really does feel that good.

"Are you about to flash us your O-face while your nipples continue to squirt milk onto the floor?" Winnie teased.

"It could very well be a possibility."

"I think this massage room is tainted now," Georgia said. "They're going to have to burn it to the ground. Too much weirdness has occurred in the past thirty minutes."

"Don't light the matches until my boobs stop flowing. I'd prefer not to have to sprint out of this room with milk shooting out of my nipples. Eduardo has already spent far too much time rearranging bottles for the day."

"So it wasn't just me, then?" Winnie asked. "I thought that man had spent an outrageous amount of time moving around like three bottles of massage oil. I was starting to get concerned I was seeing shit."

Georgia laughed. "Pretty sure it was Cassie's dining offer that flustered him a bit."

"A bit?" Winnie laughed. "How about next time you refrain from offering to breastfeed the staff?"

"Does this rule only apply to massages?" I asked.

"You are deranged."

I laughed. "Thanks, Wheorgie. I love you too. Make sure Kline slicks down his rain jacket before heading out into the backwoods."

She groaned. "I'm never going to hear the end of that, am I?"

"Nope," Winnie and I both responded without a second thought.

CHAPTER 11

Wes

The door closed with a slam that startled me awake from dreams that were part nightmare. My eyes searched the panes of the ceiling as I tried to get my bearings and figure out where the fuck I was and what I was doing there.

After Winnie and Georgia had left and the pageant started, things turned pretty quickly to my version of hell.

Thatch, with his mini-me strapped to his chest, mocked every single one of my players as they tried to turn themselves into dancers in the name of the opening number of the pageant. Rollins had rhythm, and Sean Phillips looked like you could drop him right in the middle of anything—preparation that was no doubt at least in part thanks to his sister—but Jeremy Overshaw and Deshaun Littleton were the complete opposite of okay.

They swayed to the music and shuffled their feet, but their timing was off, and every time they had to do anything to actually lead their partner, they ended up hindering them. It was a spectacle that had the audience laughing instead of watching in awe, and Thatch didn't waste the opportunity to run his mouth constantly.

"Oh, sneakers," he'd announced, leaning down to Ace to point out Overshaw's flaws. *"Did you see that? I think he almost decapitated her."*

I'd tried to tune him out, but when amusing bumbles turned to anarchy, the difficult task became impossible.

"He's down!" Thatch had nearly yelled as Littleton and the girl he was escorting hit the stage floor with a thud. He dropped his voice to that of a sports announcer and ran down the play-by-play helpfully as I jumped to my feet in fear that one of my best players had gone down during the Miss Teen USA pageant rather than in a fucking game. *"He steps back out of the pocket and shuffles, but oh, here she comes out of the backfield, Little Miss Muffet breaking through the line and bringing him down for a loss of five yards and just about all of his pride."* Ace, an apple picked right from his father's tree, apparently, even squealed in agreement, a giggle of glee piercing the air.

The kid couldn't even hold his fucking head up, and already he was helping Thatch mock my players—and by extension, me.

I was already pulling out my phone to dial Winnie, but Thatch had reached over to stop me when Littleton jumped back to his feet with no injury other than his pink-tinged cheeks, courtesy of embarrassment.

And then the music had picked right back up where it left off like nothing even happened. Thanks to taping delays, when it aired on TV, they'd probably plan to edit it together, and no one would ever be the wiser.

And if not, I'd have Georgia see that they did, whether it was part of the plan or not. Littleton would be forever grateful.

Another smash from the main room made me push up to my elbows and pay attention. I knew Lexi could sleep through almost anything, so I wasn't too worried about her.

And I do mean that literally. The fire alarm went off during some late-night cookie baking just before coming here—apparently, Winnie had promised them to Quinn for the trip, and yes, I'm rolling my eyes too.

I took off at a sprint headed for Lexi's room, but she never even fucking shifted. And trust me, that thing is fucking loud.

But it wasn't like Winnie to come in so noisily—she had a kid, after all—and I'd completely lost track of the time.

I caught a glimpse of the clock just as she came stumbling through the door of our bedroom, heels dangling precariously from one finger.

Three a.m.

"God, sweetheart," I said as I sat halfway up and rubbed at my eyes. "You're just getting back?"

She dropped her shoes to the floor and pulled her dress directly over her head, and I decided it was time to stop talking. There'd be plenty of time for questions later, when she wasn't stripping her clothes off and crawling toward me and—goddamn—she was drunk.

Sweet merciful heaven, drunk sex with Winnie Winslow was going to be amazing.

She bit her lip and climbed up the bed until her hips straddled mine, her hair cascading wildly down and around her shoulders.

She reached behind herself to unhook her bra and pulled it down before tossing it to the side. Nipples peaked and pink, her skin seemed to glow in the low light of the moon reflecting off of the ocean that poured through the window.

Her hands came to my cheeks as she spoke in a cheeky whisper. "You don't look like an Irritated Owl right now." I pushed my fingertips deeper into the exposed skin at her hips and swallowed.

"No," I agreed roughly. "I am not even a little bit irritated."

"Me either," she replied, her eyes lighting up. My heart tripped inside my chest at the brightness inside of them. It was much more potent than it used to be and rooted far deeper.

She looked like a different woman than she had just months ago, and I felt like maybe I was at least a little responsible for that. Loving her, loving Lexi, being the best support system I could be for both of them. I put the emphasis of all my efforts on one simple question.

"Good massage, baby?"

She nodded and bit minutely into her lip, her forehead falling easily against mine. Her cheek pulled up and a mini dimple formed like an extension of the corner of her mouth. Like her lips weren't quite big enough to contain her whole smile.

"The best. There was a minor snafu with Cassie almost breast-feeding the masseuse, but all ended well and we decided to go dancing." She sat up and undulated back and forth to imaginary music, her breasts swaying magically with every move.

I didn't even bother questioning the Cassie scenario. Nothing surprised me when it came to her level of insanity.

But good God. My gorgeous girl and her delicious fucking tits.

My hands slid up the sides of her ribcage almost without permission. Not that I didn't want them to, but I really no longer had any control. "Oh, yeah?"

"Mmhmm," she hummed with a nod, closing her eyes and letting her head drop back.

"Do you love me?" she asked softly.

"Oh, Win. You have no idea."

Her head came forward, and her playful eyes found mine. "Are you tired?"

Back and forth, I forced my head to shake slowly. "No, baby," I whispered softly, finally filling my palm with the flesh of her breast and rubbing a soft thumb across her responsive nipple.

"Do you want to make me feel good?"

She gasped as I sat up quickly and pulled her hips tight to mine and our chests skin-to-skin. "Always."

Each point on the trail of her jaw felt like silk under my lips, and the smell of her arousal taunted me from below. I followed its suggested path, hitting all of Winnie's most sensitive spots as I went, down the line of her jaw, right to the spot behind her ear, around the side of her throat, along the bone at her collar and right to the center of her chest, pushing her to lean back and give me access as I went.

She didn't contest anything, moaning and closing her eyes at the first hit of my lips to her throat.

"You are the most amazing woman," I murmured to the space in between her breasts, a place I would happily live if she let me.

"Wes," she whined, and I smiled, nibbling at the inside of both mounds of supple flesh.

"You want me to be sweet or rough, sweetheart?" I asked, and her already arched back flared more.

"Both."

Perfect answer.

I picked her body up from my lap and swung my legs out of the way, before setting her back down on the bed. She gasped, far too impressed with the maneuver thanks to the help of the alcohol, and I nearly wept in excitement.

She pushed up on her elbows to look at me, but I stopped her progress with a soft hand on her chest and a kiss to the corner of her mouth. "Lie back and spread your legs."

A shiver wracked her body as I went on. "I'm absolutely dying to eat your pussy."

She whimpered and I smiled, climbing from the bed, much to her confusion.

Worry creased her forehead, but I put a finger to my lips in command as she opened her mouth. "Lie back," I repeated. "And spread those beautiful legs. I'm just closing the door."

She rotated around to face me as I moved and did as I asked, dropping to her back with a soft bounce and settling her heels into the comforter about three feet apart.

Hands to her knees and my own knee to the bed, I commanded, "Wider."

She moaned with the effort to do what I asked and jumped as I grabbed the sides of her sheer panties and ripped them apart.

"Oh, God," she cried.

"Are you wet, Win?"

Her head bounced up and down, and her eyes closed with heaviness. "Touch me."

Powerless to deny her, I sank to my elbows, face in front of heaven, and ran two fingers from right above her clit all the way to the sensitive skin right above her asshole.

She loved when I played with her ass just a little, an obviously untapped area from her previous lovers, and I felt nearly high from her reaction every time.

Down the insides of her thighs, from her knees to the crease where leg turned into something else, I rubbed my hands, trailing a wet shine from top to bottom on the right one.

"See that?" I asked, and she nodded even though her eyes were closed.

"No, baby," I said with a chuckle. "Open your eyes."

She did, so I ran two fingers down the trail to call her attention to it once again. "All that is because you love me."

She nodded even though I hadn't asked a question.

"And you know I'm going to make you feel good."

"Wes."

"What, baby?" I asked. "Don't want to wait?"

She shook her head almost violently, and with an answer as sound as that, I couldn't even fathom the idea of denying her.

I leaned down and sucked the skin just below her belly button straight into my mouth, circling my tongue around it and humming on her taste. "Appetizer tastes good."

She moaned and writhed a little, grabbing at the comforter on both sides and pushing her flesh farther into my mouth.

"I bet the entrée is going to be even better."

"Please," she whispered.

Down the bed, I settled onto my chest and threw her legs over my shoulders, licking a path along the now drying trail I'd created moments ago.

She couldn't do anything more than whimper, the longing and

alcohol finally mixing into something she no longer had any control over.

I rubbed two fingers around the edges of her clit before giving it a bump and watching as more excitement flooded the space below. With practiced ease, I pulled it up and around, coating the little nub with just the right flavor for my mouth.

"Mm," I breathed, inhaling and closing my lips around the carefully placed moisture. I was never prepared for how good she was going to taste, and as a result, I pretty much immediately lost my mind and myself to the moment, eating at her with an intensity that didn't build or dawdle, two fingers curling inside to rub at the spot that always pleased her while my other hand teased her asshole, now soaked with arousal.

She gasped and grabbed at my hair, pushing my face into her harder and forcing me to eat more. I thought my erection would punch through the bed if I didn't fuck her soon.

And I needed to for more reasons for that.

I could see in her eyes that she'd be done as soon as her orgasm washed out, completely spent and comatose in a way that only a totally satisfied woman could be.

I broke the suction seal of my mouth, and she cried out.

"Don't worry, baby. I promise I've got more for you."

She nodded as I stood back and shoved my shorts off of my hips before climbing onto the bed and rubbing myself through the mess I'd left.

"Wes," she whispered, and I smiled, leaning forward, pushing myself inside and rubbing my nose against hers.

"I love you too, Fred."

She nodded, tiny tears reflecting in her eyes as I pushed my way home over and over again, perfecting the angle so that I rubbed against her clit with every move.

She looked poised to explode—tight, clenched eyes and open mouth, and I knew I had to hurry. But it wasn't really any effort at all, she had me so worked up, and when she fell over the hill and squeezed me inside, I toppled right along with her.

Breathing heavily on top of her, I noticed the exact moment she faded away and fell sound asleep in my arms, my cock still inside of her.

I pulled out gently and brushed the hair from her flushed face before burying my face in the space between her shoulder and head.

I didn't want to leave—ever.

So I did the exact opposite, climbing from the bed, tiptoeing into the bathroom to clean up, and then padding to the side table by the bed and opening the drawer.

It sat there, right on top, and I didn't even hesitate before reaching in, opening the box, and pulling it out.

The bed squeaked only a little as I put a knee into it and reached for the delicate hand resting above her head and took care of business.

Carefully lifting her body up and pulling the covers down, I settled her inside and climbed in behind her to fall asleep happier than I'd ever been—linking our hands and hearts forever.

CHAPTER 12

Winnie

Warmth cocooned me, and I had the urge to purr like a kitten from my cozy spot inside Wes's arms. I had no idea what time it was, but when I fluttered my eyes open, no rogue ray of light pierced their sensitive receptors. The sun hadn't risen yet, and upon closer inspection, I realized the first hello of sun was still a little way off. Utter darkness still concealed the picturesque view behind the flowy white curtains of our hotel bedroom.

With unfocused eyes, I scanned from one piece of furniture to the next to find our clothes not only dangling from each one but also scattered across the floor in haphazard displays in between. Wes's pants mingled with my dress, and the scraps of my underwear lay tattered to the side. I blushed at the reminder of just how badly I had needed Wes last night. What started as a mission to cheer the glum version of our friend Georgia up had turned into wild, uninhibited, highly vulgar dancing and one too many glasses of sangria. Hell, maybe *two* too many. Pain pierced my brain as I tried to sit up.

Shit. Yeah. Two too many.

Well past two a.m., I'd stumbled my way back to my hotel room,

horny and needy and ready to do just about anything to seduce Wes
into getting dirty and naked with me. I'd come up with an entire list
on the elevator ride to the top, including something with my boobs
and a complicated twist that my now sober, though hungover brain
could no longer process.

Thankfully, seeing as I'd forgotten more than ninety percent of
the things on the list by the time I finally figured out how to make
the keycard open the door to the room, the seduction hadn't required
much effort.

God, I love this man.

He'd given me everything I had needed and craved and was so
desperate for, *plus* so much more. Moments. Memories. Pleasure,
both as expected physically *and* all the way in my soul. And that was
quite a feat with a woman who couldn't do much more than remember her own name, five sheets to the wind, and even more glasses of
fruity wine deep.

We hadn't just fucked until we both got off. No. There wasn't an
inch of skin left untouched, an ounce of me unloved—and I was certain that was my definition of heaven. Wes loving me and me loving
Wes until we couldn't feel any single thing but each other.

I'd do just about anything to have that for forever.

Wes stirred a little in his sleep, a groan and a deep inhalation in
the hair at my neck just two of the things I loved most about our position, and I smiled. He was wrapped around me like a second skin,
his arms holding me tightly and his warm, muscular body spooning
me from behind.

Curious about the time, I carefully reached out with my left hand
to tilt the alarm clock on the nightstand in my direction. The glow-
ing numbers on the little black screen were an afterthought when my
eyes caught sight of my ring finger.

Oh. My. God.

I blinked several times just to make sure what I was seeing was
real and then forced them apart when the morning-after dry eye got

the better of me.

This was the absolutely wrong time to lose the ability of sight.

Eyes thankfully open, I held my left hand out in front of me and just stared.

My reaction was supremely delayed, but when cognitive function finally caught up to what I was seeing, a gasp left my lungs in a hard whoosh and my heart fought to pound its way out of my chest.

Oh.

My.

God.

There was a *ring* on my finger.

The most beautiful, classic, sparkly, and gorgeous diamond solitaire ring sat on my left ring finger, and *I* hadn't fucking put it there. More than that, I didn't recollect anyone else doing it either.

I racked my brain for details of last night and couldn't recall anything besides the massage and the dancing and the drinks and the gloriously naked Wes rocking my world into mind-blowing orgasms and then black peace—the last orgasm apparently had been so powerful it lulled me straight to sleep.

Aside from the details, and the hows and whys of what it was doing there, it was literally the ring of my dreams. If I could've created a Pinterest board with the exact particulars of my dream engagement ring, this pretty baby would have been it.

How in the hell did this perfect fucking ring get here?

I felt Wes stir awake behind me, and his arms tightened around my waist. His chin dug into the soft divot of my shoulder. "Morning, sweetheart," he greeted with a raspy, sleep-filled voice.

But I didn't respond. *Couldn't* respond. I could only stare in surprise and awe and downright amazement at my left hand spread painfully wide in front of me.

"You're my life, Winnie Winslow," Wes whispered into my ear, sliding his hand along the top of my arm and then curling around the bottom so that his palm met mine. "You and Lex are my whole life, and I don't want to go another day without knowing that you are my wife and Lexi is my daughter. I want to love you both every single day for the rest of forever. I want to be both of your shoulders to lean on. I want to be your biggest supporter. I want to be your everything because you, my beautiful girl, are *my* everything."

He pulled me around to face him, sides to the bed and faces only inches apart. Nose-to-nose and eyes locked so tight it felt physical, nothing could've broken our focus on one another.

"Last night, lying there asleep with a blush still tinting your satisfied cheeks, you were so close to my version of perfect, it hurt. I put that ring on your finger, and all the pain and any hint of almost went completely away. You were perfect. You *are* perfect. Will you marry me, Winnie Winslow?"

I searched his hazel gaze, and the only thing that was staring back at me was a man, a *beautiful* man, with his heart on his sleeve and the promise of forever in his eyes. Slowly, softly, and without restraint, I felt myself, my heart, my soul, be consumed by an infinite amount of love. And I knew there was only one answer to his question.

No doubts.

No fears.

Just… "Yes." I nodded as tears started to stream down my cheeks.

He took my left hand in his and brought it up to his lips, kissing my ring gently all the while his eyes smiled into mine. I felt my heart grow two sizes bigger inside of my chest.

"I love you so much," I whispered through the tears clogging my throat. This man, this amazing, perfectly imperfect man, had just asked me to marry him. He had been so desperate to be my husband and couldn't wait another day, another hour, another minute, that he had put the engagement ring on my finger while I was asleep.

It was a little presumptive, but fuck, he wanted to be mine for the rest of his life.

I couldn't really complain about that.

And it was a certainty that I wanted to be his for the rest of mine.

"I love you too, Win." His lips melded themselves to mine, and my soon-to-be *husband* kissed with me all of the tenderness and passion and love I had ever felt in my entire life.

We stayed like that for what felt like a blissful eternity, simply holding one another and kissing. Good God, there was so much kissing. Not rushed, not hurried to lead to other things like we harried adults so often did—just pure and sweet and tender kisses. I closed my eyes and fell into his lips' loving embrace. *Heavenly.*

"Let's get married today," he whispered against my mouth.

My eyes popped open, and I leaned back to look into his still smiling gaze.

"What? *Today?*"

He nodded. "Yes. Today. Let's get married, Win. Right now."

I giggled. "It's like five in the morning, Wes. I'm not sure that we *can* get married right now."

"Oh, it's possible," he said with a giant grin. *Ah, right.* I guess when you were a freaking *billionaire*, all sorts of things were possible. "Let's get married right now, on the beach, with just you, Lex, and me."

I was awed. "You're serious?"

"One hundred percent serious."

I cut a nervous laugh short and asked again—just for confirmation. "You want to get married on the beach? Right now? Just the three of us?"

He nodded, smiling bigger than I had ever seen him. "That is *exactly* what I want."

"I don't have a dress…or shoes…or—"

Wes's smile grew bigger, breaking his all-time record immediately, and he placed his fingers over my lips. "Baby, if you want it, I'll make sure you get it. But I promise, you don't need any of it. You're literally the most beautiful thing I have ever seen right here, right now, and that's all I need—you and Lex for forever. The rest is inconsequential."

God, this man… I was so in love with him it should have been illegal. Heck, maybe it was. I'd just be sure to get moving, get fucking up, and get married—quickly enough that the cops wouldn't catch me.

Because *he* was the one who was perfect. *For me.*

I grinned against his fingertips. "Okay."

His hazel eyes lit up, and he lifted his hand off of my mouth. "Okay?"

"Let's do it. Let's get married right now, on the beach."

He pressed a smacking and playful kiss to my lips. "I love you so much."

I smiled. "I love you too."

A second later he was hopping off the bed and tossing on a pair of boxer briefs. "Get up, get dressed," he demanded impatiently.

I giggled, watching him scramble around the room for clothes. "In a hurry much?"

"Fuck yes, I'm in a hurry." He flashed a wink in my direction. "The most beautiful and amazing woman on the planet has just agreed to marry me. You can bet your sweet little ass I'm not letting her change her mind, and if it's going to happen in time for sunrise, I've got to get a fucking move on."

A little over an hour later, as the sun started to crest above the water line, we stood on the beach, barefoot and dressed in pajamas, ready to get married.

Lex stood between us with messy pigtails in her hair and the biggest smile I had ever seen on her cute little face.

"Do you mind if we say our own vows?" Wes asked the minister who stood before us. Somehow, my very, very soon-to-be husband had managed to find a minister who was staying at the resort and more than willing to come out to the beach at six thirty in the morning so two crazy and in love people could get married.

My eyes went wide for a beat. "Vows? You wrote vows?" I asked Wes on a whisper. *I have no fucking vows.*

He chuckled softly. "Don't worry, sweetheart. I've got all three of us covered."

I had no idea what he meant by that, but before I could question further, the minister chimed in and said, "Of course," with a genuine smile on his lips.

Wes picked Lexi up and turned toward me. "Do you have the rings?" he whispered into her ear.

She giggled and nodded her little head before slipping her fingers into the shirt pocket of her Minions pajamas and pulling out two simple and classic gold wedding bands.

Wes's eyes met mine, and I couldn't look at anything or anyone else. He held my left hand in his while my daughter stayed on his hip, hands wrapped around his neck like a monkey.

"Winifred Winslow, as I stand here before you, my eyes looking so deeply into your big blue ones, I see all of the things I fell in love with. Wild hair, sassy spirit, and so much intelligence it hurts."

I shook my head but said nothing as he went on.

"As I stand here before you, my heart beating so loudly in my ears that it echoes like it's actually mixing with yours, I find myself lost for the right words to say."

My heart sped up, and I gulped down a swallow, my hand spasming in his.

"As I stand here before you, this endless ring in my hand, it makes me remember how infinitely complete you make my life.

"With every smile, every embrace."

I smiled, longing for his embrace.

"It makes me remember how blessed and lucky I really am. It makes me remember every laugh we've ever shared, every hard time we made it through together, and every beautiful moment there is to come."

For the first time in a long time, the future looked blindingly bright.

"Do you, Winnie, take me as your husband?" Wes asked.

My vision blurred slightly as tears coated my eyes. "Yes. I do."

He looked at Lex. "Can I have Mommy's ring?"

She nodded, placing the smaller of the two gold bands into his palm.

Wes slowly slid the gold ring onto my finger while his eyes gazed into mine. "Winnie, I give you this ring, my heart, my soul. I give you everything I am today and the more I hope to be tomorrow. I promise to love you, protect you, be with you forever, and cherish every moment with you as if it was the last moment on earth." He smiled down at me and then kissed the ring on my finger.

"Okay, Lexi, now hand Mommy my ring."

She reached out her hand and placed the remaining gold band into my hand.

"Will you let me be your husband, Winnie?" Wes asked and held out his left hand for me. "Will you let me love you forever?"

I felt decidedly less impressive as I answered with a simple, "Yes."

I took his hand in mine and gently slid the band onto his finger. "I love you," I whispered and kissed the ring on his finger like he had done with mine.

He smiled with tears coating his eyes. "I love you too."

"And, ditto. To all the other stuff you said," I said with a bite of my lip. "I'll do all that too."

Even the minister laughed.

Wes set Lexi on her feet and kneeled before my little girl. He slipped a small little gold band from his pocket and took her right hand in his. He smiled up into her big brown eyes with so much love and affection I felt my heart migrate into my throat.

"My pretty little Lexi, will you let me be your daddy forever and ever and ever?"

She giggled and nodded her head.

He slid a tiny gold band onto her right ring finger and pulled her into a tight hug, kissing her forehead with love etched all the way to the corners of his face.

I knew for a fact I bore the same marks on my heart.

CHAPTER 13

Kline

Pulling Georgie closer to me in the elevator, I buried my face in her throat and sighed. I didn't even notice that both of my hands had gone to her stomach and settled there until she tentatively placed her hands on top of mine. It was still fairly early, but there was no pin in the world sharp enough to pop my hot air balloon of fucking rapture.

I knew Georgia was happy but nervous, but I felt like that was finally something I could handle. All this time spent unable to do anything for her heartbreak, with absolutely nothing reassuring to tell her, made this obstacle seem far less formidable.

Her fear was real and founded, but so was the pregnancy and everything it meant for the two of us. She was pregnant—with our baby.

We'd spent nothing less than a metaphorical eternity imagining it, and still, I'd never quite pinpointed the actual sensation of this feeling. Probably because it wasn't possible, just like you can't understand the connection with your child until you hold him or her.

I absolutely couldn't wait for that moment, looking down into the tiny bundle in my arms and seeing her mother there or marveling at the reflection of myself in him.

I had a long time to wait, so I'd been entertaining myself with the thing that always served as my most favorite hobby—my wife.

The ping of the elevator echoed inside my head as Georgia giggled and pulled me forward, my front still practically plastered to her back as she headed for the little restaurant where we usually had breakfast.

It'd only been days, but it was human nature to fall into a habit as if you'd be there forever. To find comfort in routine and regularity as a way to mimic your everyday life—the very life you were trying to escape by being on vacation.

"God," I murmured as I kissed on my wife's shoulder and pulled her closer as we walked side by side.

"Kline!" she chastised without force or derision. She liked what I was doing just as much as I did, so I kept doing it, concentrating on nothing more than her and putting one foot in front of the other.

Distracted by Georgia's neck and Georgia's ass and Georgia's laugh, I didn't notice the motley crew at the table until it was too late. My wife had pulled away with a smile, and I moved to sit down across from her without even glancing at anything other than her face.

Only a tap on my shoulder brought my eyes around.

"Ah, Jesus," I cried as I pulled back up from almost sitting in Thatch's lap.

"Hey, dude. I get it. I'd be into me too," Thatch rambled as he continued to smother his pancakes in butter. I waved him off with a very particular finger and moved to the other side of the table.

He pretended to take offense, but the smirk in his eyes and on his mouth kind of gave him away. "But I'm a—" he started.

"Father now," everyone recited in unison. He'd been saying it so goddamn much, I was starting to have dreams about hearing it. Apparently, everyone else felt the same.

"We get it," Wes added with a laugh, but Thatch was pretty much unfazed. He was always unflappable like that when everyone got riled and reacted in some way, because that was his goal in the first place. He didn't feel shame like normal people, and he certainly didn't care to fit into societal norms.

It was one of my favorite things about him. That, and, ironically, the fact that he was a father now—and a good one.

Butterflies took flight in my stomach at the reminder that I'd soon be able to say the same thing, and I couldn't stop the resulting smile from swallowing my face. Of course, someone had to notice.

"What are you smiling about, Big-dick?" Cassie asked.

Unbidden and completely unplanned, I blurted, "Georgia's pregnant."

It was so unlike me. But then again, I'd never been expecting a baby before.

Everyone froze, even Georgia at my side, and I winced at the fact that I hadn't even consulted her on the decision to share our news. Fuck, I hadn't even consulted myself. There'd basically been no thought involved at all—just emotion.

"Kline," she whispered and turned to me. I only had eyes for her.

"I'm sorry, baby," I apologized on a whisper. "I'm just happy."

She closed her eyes then, one tear spilling from the corner of her eye and nearly breaking me in two.

"I don't get it," I heard Wes stage-whisper.

Lexi didn't bother to lower her volume. "Statistically, married couples are usually happy with the news that they've conceived."

"Dude," Thatch whispered. "She's so smart."

Winnie smiled and put a hand to Georgia's shoulder. "Are you okay?"

One deep breath and my wife finally returned. She'd conquered the madness inside and convinced herself to share the rest.

"I'm fine," she answered Winnie, but her eyes were on me. I leaned forward and touched my lips to hers.

Steeling her spine, she turned to the group and started to explain. "We've…had trouble…getting pregnant."

"Wheorgie," Cassie whispered, the pain in her friend's voice hitting her somewhere deep. "Was this the big secret?"

Georgia nodded. "But we're finally pregnant. Apparently." She shrugged. "I'm having some trouble believing it."

"How many weeks along are you?" Winnie asked.

"Eleven or so," I offered when Georgia stayed silent a beat too long.

Thatch spoke around a mouthful of pancake, shrugging his beefy shoulder and shaking his head mockingly. "So fucking find a doctor and get an ultrasound and make your wife feel better, for fuck's sake."

That was actually a good idea. From Thatch. He honestly had good ideas more than I'd like to admit. The whole world was upside down and he was a maniac, but at the end of the day, he was one of the best kind of people to have in your corner.

"Christ," he muttered, stabbing another bite. "It's like I have to do all the husband coaching."

Cassie nodded supportively. "You should give classes."

"I don't know," Winnie whispered quietly, running her hand through Wes's messy hair. "Some people seem to have a pretty good handle on it all on their own."

My eyes narrowed immediately before zooming in and refocusing to their interwoven hands on the table.

Jackpot.

"Something you'd like to share with the class?" I asked through a smirk, jerking my head to the sparkling metal on each of their most significant fingers.

"They got married this morning," Lexi shared without prompting, and all eyes went to her. She wilted slightly under the scrutiny, so I turned back to the matter—and people—at hand.

"Oh, really?"

"And we weren't fluffing invited?" Cassie whisper-raged. Ace slept comfortably on her shoulder, and even Crazy Cassie knew not to wake a sleeping baby.

"It was just us," Winnie said quietly, and Cassie rolled her eyes. Everyone else looked on, bouncing back and forth, as they volleyed their little war.

"Obviously." Her voice was rough with the effort it took to stay quiet. "But it could have been just *us*." She waved a hand in a circle around the table.

"I know, but—"

"But nothing!" Cassie whisper-yelled, and Wes's face turned stern in a way that even Thatch took it seriously.

"Cass—"

I waded in and shut them all up with the one question I thought held all the answers. "How was it, Lex?"

All eyes turned to our friends' perfect, brilliant little girl.

She shrugged shyly before whispering, "Good. I'm Wes's daughter now. I'll have to check to make sure he filed the right paperwork, but ceremonially anyway."

Six big fucking mouths, and in that moment, you could have heard a pin drop.

"Well, all right," Thatch said roughly, a lump in even his big-ass throat. It must have taken a hell of a lot of emotion to clog the monstrous thing.

"Come on, Crazy," he murmured to Cassie, pulling Ace gently from her arms and placing him against his own beefy shoulder. "Let's go for a walk on the beach before ultrasound time."

Georgia's eyebrows shot together. "Um…"

"You'll let us know what time?" Thatch asked, and I sat back, straightening in my chair.

"I will," Winnie noted before I could open my mouth. Then she turned to Wes and her eyes were moony. "Let's go for a walk too."

I had a feeling Melinda would be on duty and "a walk" was really innuendo for another form of exercise. Hell, it probably was for Thatch and Cassie too.

As the table cleared and we were left sitting there alone, Georgie's head settled on my shoulder and she sighed. "Is my ultrasound really going to be a freaking group activity?"

Everyone sure thought it was going to be, but that was completely inconsequential as far as I was concerned. Serious, I told her the only answer that mattered. "Only if you want it to be."

She was silent for several beats before finally shrugging. "Actually, with this group, for some reason, it kind of seems right."

CHAPTER 14

Georgia

Prone on the bed and waiting to find out one of the most important things in my life, I looked up and found seven sets of eyes staring directly at my exposed stomach. Mom, Dad, and seventy of their closest friends looking on, waiting to see the first picture of their baby.

Okay, so maybe it wasn't seventy, but with how much square footage Thatcher Kelly filled out, you'd have thought it was.

Nerves flitted inside of my stomach before crawling slowly out the length of my arms and legs. And when Cassie lifted up her shirt and blew out her stomach forcefully in jest, I had the strong and irrational urge to hop off the bed and run out of the room.

Fear was a prominent emotion swirling inside of my veins, but that didn't stop my friends from being their ridiculous selves. In fact, they probably thought acting crazy would calm me, distract me, even, but I was way past the point of help.

I was absolutely terrified that we wouldn't see what we were so desperate to see on the ultrasound. I had been trying so hard not to get attached until I knew for certain that I was pregnant, that there was a beautiful little baby growing inside of me. I had been trying so hard not to get my hopes up, not to feel the love and joy inside my heart, but now, with everyone here and nowhere to hide, it was useless. I wanted this baby, *our baby,* more than I had ever wanted anything in my entire life, and if disappointment rained down on us today, there wouldn't be a person out there who would miss that I was fucking soaked.

God, please, let it be real. Please let this be a healthy pregnancy. Please, please, please…

I shut my eyes and tried like hell to force the tears floating behind my lids back. I was afraid if I let the dam truly burst, there wouldn't be soft cries or a delicate sniffle—I would be wrecked, fucking ravaged by full-on sobs. And I wouldn't have any control over how long they lasted. The emotional roller coaster Kline and I had been on during the past several months had taken its toll on me.

I felt my husband's hand wrap around mine, and I found the strength to open my eyes and meet his loving gaze. "I love you," he mouthed.

"I love you too," I mouthed back.

"Okay, Georgia, I'm just going to put this gooey and most likely cold stuff on your belly and see if we can see your baby on the abdominal ultrasound," Dr. Shay instructed. She was an OB/GYN on staff at a hospital nearby and, thankfully, had been more than willing to make a house call to our hotel room, with her ultrasound machine in tow.

"Since you're a little over eleven weeks, I think we have a good shot of being able to see the baby, but I don't want you to get worried if that's not the case," she continued as she slid on latex gloves. "Sometimes, we need to do a vaginal ultrasound to really get a good picture."

"Um…vaginal ultrasound?" I asked with wide eyes and glanced around the room at the various faces of our friends, all of which were pointed directly at me.

"Oh, don't worry, Wheorgie," Cassie chimed in. "We'll cover our eyes if she has to shove anything up your vag."

Winnie laughed and shook her head. "No, we won't cover our eyes, we will leave the room and give her privacy."

Cassie's face scrunched up in annoyance. "Speak for yourself. I'm staying. I've seen her vagina anyway."

"No, you have not!" I exclaimed, and Cassie quirked a brow. "Shut up," I muttered when I recalled the home Brazilian wax debacle during college. I hadn't been able to walk straight for a good week after that.

"Anyway," Cassie continued. "I think you have a very pretty pussay. I can understand Kline's fascination with it."

"I'm a female, and I have a vagina," Lexi leisurely announced to the room. "The vagina is a muscular and tubular part of the female genital tract which, in female humans, extends from the vulva to the cervix. The outer vaginal opening may be partly covered by a membrane called the hymen. The vagina allows for sexual intercourse and childbirth and channels menstrual flow."

Various reactions flew through the room at the words sexual intercourse and menstrual flow leaving a six-year-old girl's mouth.

Kline smirked down at me in amusement.

Wes choked on saliva and started coughing.

Thatch and Cassie burst into laughter, startling a sleeping Ace to cry softly for a moment on his dad's shoulder before drifting back into dreamland.

"Um, sweetie," Winnie said as she picked Lex up into her arms. "Where did you learn that?"

"Netter's *Atlas of Human Anatomy*."

Winnie raised a brow. "You've been reading my books from med school?"

Lexi nodded. "Uh-huh. I can tell you a lot more about the vagina. Do you want to hear, Mommy?"

"Yes, please, I'd love to hear more about it," Thatch announced. "One of my favorite subjects."

"Jesus," Wes muttered, and Kline and I both laughed.

"How about you tell me all about it later?" Winnie smartly redirected before things got out of hand.

"Okay, Mommy," Lexi agreed.

"Ready?" Dr. Shay asked as she sat on the edge of the bed beside my hip, her hand confidently holding the ultrasound probe.

I mentally scolded the nerves in my belly and forced a smile and a nod. They'd better get out of the way because I didn't want to see them. I wanted to see my baby. Kline squeezed my hand as he noticed the change in me.

"Okay, let's see your baby," she said with a smile and squirted three blobs of ultrasound gel onto my stomach.

She placed the probe onto my skin and started to rotate it around in circles, and Kline's hand's grip grew tighter on my mine. I had to shut my eyes to stop myself from bursting into tears.

"Oh, here we go," Dr. Shay announced, but I still couldn't find the strength to open my eyes. Here we go could have been anything. Here we go could have been bad news. Here we go could have been…

"Would you like to hear your baby's heartbeat, Georgia?"

My baby's heartbeat?

My eyes popped open, and I let out the breath of air I didn't realize I was holding tightly in my lungs. Wes and Thatch high-fived behind their women, and Cassie covered her mouth with a hand.

"Would you?" Dr. Shay asked again. I forced myself to stop looking at my friends and see her. The happiness in her eyes. The *good news* that lived there.

I nodded.

She reached toward the ultrasound machine with her free hand and tapped a few buttons, and then the room was filled with the steady and strong whooshing sounds of a little heart beating.

It was the most beautiful sound I had ever heard in my entire life. Half of Kline. Half of me. All of our love wrapped up in one tiny little package.

Kline had tears in his eyes as he stared at the ultrasound screen in absolute awe. I followed his gaze and, for the first time ever, I saw *our* baby. Its tiny face and his or her little heart, a bright spot on the screen fluttering like a hummingbird's wing.

"There's your baby, Georgia," Dr. Shay said with a smile. "Everything looks healthy and strong. I'd say you are around eleven weeks and three days, but once you get back home, your doctor will be able to do a vaginal ultrasound and give you exact dates and gestation."

I couldn't hold back the tears after that, and I didn't even try. They streamed down my cheeks in a steady flow of relief and all-consuming and unconditional love.

Our baby.

"That's our baby, Kline," I whispered in amazement. "Right there, on the screen, that's our baby."

He smiled, and two tears slowly slipped from the corner of his eye and down his jaw. "Our healthy and strong baby."

I glanced around the room at our best friends and saw their faces mirroring our joy. They were happy for us. So very happy for us. And for the first time, maybe ever, they were quiet. Letting us have this.

Wes smiled a genuine smile and wrapped his arm around Winnie's shoulder, tucking her into his side. "Congratulations, guys."

"I'm so happy for you, Georgie," Cassie said softly, all of our years of friendship a slideshow in her voice.

I honestly didn't think I had ever experienced a more beautiful moment than this one.

Love.

Both inside of me and all around—and so very obviously unending.

CHAPTER 15

Thatch

"Cass!" I called out in a loud whisper as the door to the room shut behind me. I'd been for a run on the beach with Kline and Wes a couple of hours after the ultrasound, as Georgia, finally at peace, got some rest. I'd been gone for no more than an hour and a half, but I was more than ready for some time with my woman and baby.

It was weird to feel so contently dependent on their company and daily nurturing, but they gave me something that I couldn't give myself, no matter how good I was at everything. And let's be real, I *was* good at everything.

But as much as I loved myself, there was a vast difference between that and the love of another, someone you loved with your entire being. All I wanted was to have their love in return, so getting it felt all that much more rewarding. I wanted to love myself, but that wasn't a challenge.

Slowly, knowing enough about life with a baby to be quiet after not getting an immediate answer to my call, I worked my way through the suite until coming to the room we'd been using as Ace's nursery away from home. It was actually the bigger of the two bedrooms, but the sun didn't blast straight through the windows in the morning and it was the farthest from the hall.

I could hear the soft sounds of Ace's sleeping inhalation all the way from where I was, and a premature smile formed on my face. He was one of the loudest breathing babies I'd ever encountered and a completely different animal than Frankie and Claire's Mila. She'd been a needy baby, constantly aching for attention and crying out for it with all the power in her little lungs.

Ace had more of a low-key vibe about him, as long as you were catering to his exploration of the world around him.

Two long strides brought me to the doorway. I watched, leaning into the frame, as Cassie reached up and wrapped her hand around the tiny, clutching fingers at her throat and closed her eyes.

She started to sing, no louder than a hum, really, but I knew Ace could feel the vibration of her words just fine. Skin-to-skin, chest-to-chest, he soaked every ounce of warmth and love Cassie had to give straight inside his tiny body.

Cassie's face was soft and free from the stresses of motherhood as she completely lost herself in the perfect moment.

Content baby, at ease mama, and the unbelievably beautiful picture they made for the man who loved them—I fought an unwinnable war to freeze time.

"When you're fast asleep, um, dream and lose your heartache, something something about a fluffling rainbow..."

She stumbled through the lyrics to "A Dream is a Wish Your Heart Makes," and I did my best not to laugh.

Not because it would somehow affect her delicate sensibilities, but because it might ruin my best-ever run as a voyeur.

Muted voices from the pool area below trickled up and through the window, but not enough to distract from my family in front of me. It was actually quiet in comparison to New York, markedly less hustle, bustle, and overall mayhem, and I'd lost sleep the first night while I tried to get used to it.

Of course, now that I'd gotten over the hump and was sleeping like a fetus in the fucking womb, I was sure the transition back would be even worse.

Maybe we need to move out of the city...

"What are you doing?" Cassie asked on a whisper, surprising me. I'd thought I was still under the radar, blissfully unnoticed in my perusal and enjoyment of the picture the two of them painted.

My eyes sought and held the wild maturity in hers, and I fell in love all over again.

"Watching you," I admitted, moving from the intensity of her eyes to the softness of her body. Cassie was still so honest in her individuality, perfectly consistent with the wild, crazy woman I'd fallen in love with, and yet, she'd somehow managed to deepen the softest of her dimensions and make room for the tiny little human in her arms. She didn't always do what the other moms did, but she did everything with ten times the love.

Because when Cassie held you in high regard, her affection was genuine in a way that most people only dreamed of or faked really well.

"Stalking me," she clarified with a hushed laugh, and it was one of those things that fell under past precedent. I'd always be known as the man who stalked her, and I was okay with it. Ace, safe and sound in her arms, was all the evidence I'd ever need that nothing in our past needed regret or change.

I shook my head and crossed the room, dropping to my knees in front of her chair and putting a hand to her throat and the other to the soft fluctuation of my son's breathing back.

"Loving you."

Her head tilted just slightly, into my touch, and contentment stronger than I'd ever felt before filled any hollow space in my body entirely.

"You're everything. For me, for Ace. The best wife and mother and the most interestingly intense woman I've ever met. I never know what to expect, but I never worry that I won't like it. Ace feels the same way."

"He can't talk."

"That's not what you told Georgia."

"Yeah, well, I'm a bitch and a liar."

"You are the woman we never could have dreamed."

She rolled her eyes. "I don't even know all the words to this stupid Cinderella lullaby."

I chuckled. "Maybe not. But you've got all the feelings down pat."

She pulled Ace tighter to her chest with one arm and reached one hand out to slide a finger along my neck. "Aw, baby." She laughed quietly, and it mixed with tears. "Right now, I feel numb."

"Are you—"

"In my arm. My arm is numb. Your fluffing huge kid weighs a million pounds already."

I smiled and held out my hands. "I'll take him."

"No," she denied, pulling Ace tighter to her body and my lips to hers. "I'm good right like I am."

"Me too," I agreed.

I'd be good like this for a while. *Forever.*

CHAPTER 16

Cassie

Ace huffed out a deep, content baby breath as I laid his now sleeping body down for the night and padded out toward the living area of our hotel room. The creak and whine of a shower turning on echoed from the bathroom.

I was headed for the couch when Thatch peeked his head out of the master bedroom with a sly smirk. "Want to join me, Crazy?"

Normally, I would've jumped on that kind of opportunity, but I had something I wanted to research on my laptop. Something of utmost importance, actually.

I shook my head and linked my hands together behind my back to keep them from gesturing aggressively in opposition to the mission. "Nah. I've got some work emails I need to respond to."

Lies.

Thatch flashed his most persuasive pout in my direction, but I stayed strong.

"Go take your shower, you big ogre. I'll be on the couch when you're done. Maybe we can just order some room service for dinner?"

He moved his big, muscular, and very naked frame into the

hallway on purpose, standing like a proud peacock in his birthday suit, his nipple ring winking in the lights. It shone almost obscenely, but I couldn't stop my eyes from homing in on the Supercock. It was like a magnet to my horny gaze. I actually swore it was scientifically magnetic, put there by the aliens or something, so strong was its power.

And my husband was no fool. *Goddammit.* He knew my weakness, the devious bastard.

"Are you sure, honey?" he asked with a sexy smirk. "I'll even massage your shoulders a little under the hot water…"

Oh man, he was really pulling out the big guns.

"Nope. I'm good," I bit out, even though my pussy was all but screaming, *Wait a minute! We're not good! We want the shower! We want the massage! We want the Supercock!*

"Ooooooookay," Thatch said with a wink. "Suit yourself. I'll be in the shower all wet and naked and stroking myself clean."

"Sounds like you're about to have a grand time."

I fought the urge to scowl. I wanted to have a grand time. I wanted to have a grand boning time and fuck my Jolly Green Giant in the shower, but I needed to stay focused. I had research to do, and I needed to do it while Thatch was otherwise occupied.

Thatch eyed me curiously, and I knew I had to get him out of there.

"Go take your shower and then we can order room service. I'll even let you play with my tits a little while we wait for them to deliver it."

"Fifteen minutes?" he brokered.

"I'll be generous and give you *twenty* minutes."

"A twenty-minute playdate with two of my favorite girls?"

"That's what I said."

He smirked. "Get 'em ready for Daddy. And time my shower. I've got this feeling I'm going to set some kind of world record. Actually, you better call an official from the Guinness book while you're at it."

"You got it, Daddy. Just make sure you get nice and clean so I can get you all dirty again," I taunted, grabbing both breasts and squeezing them together. His smirk turned into a full-on, megawatt smile.

The second his naked ass was out of sight, I jumped into action. I'd stupidly shortened my own clock by offering titty play, but now I had to deal with the consequences. I plopped down on the couch and set my laptop on my thighs, and as quickly as I could, found my favorite realty website and entered the criteria into the search field.

I scrolled through all of the listings and mentally approved or declined the possibilities.

Nah. That one is too big. She'd need a maid to keep it clean.

Hmmm…I bet a six-year-old would love a backyard like that. Add it to the list.

Okay…Yeah… This has a nice man cave… He'd probably love filling it with football memorabilia and other stupid shit like that…

Ohhh…This master bedroom is gorgeous… I bet they'd enjoy a sex swing in the corner of that little nook by the window…

I'd worked as quickly as I could, but I knew I was down to the wire. Luckily, I had three perfect homes saved just in the nick of time. I honestly didn't know which one would work best, but I had a feeling the options I had would make them more than happy.

"What are you doing, Crazy?"

His booming voice startled me, and I glanced up from the screen which held a picture of the last pretty house I had looked it and found Thatch leaning over the couch and practically cheek-to-cheek with me. A hand went to my chest, startled again by his close proximity this time.

"For fluff's sake," I muttered and took a deep, shaky breath. "Do you understand personal space? I mean, hell, you scared the sneakers out of me."

He tilted his head to the side and looked at me closely. "Why are you so jumpy? That's not like you."

"I'm not jumpy," I refuted.

He smirked. "You just about jumped off the couch when I asked you a question, and when you saw I was right beside you, you practically dove out the window. You're real fucking jumpy."

I scoffed and rolled my eyes. "You don't exactly have a quiet voice or a small head. When you're not expecting either of those things to be in your ear or in your face, I gotta be honest, baby, they can be fluffing terrifying."

"You don't seem to have any complaints with my big head when it's between your thighs."

"You're right," I agreed. "Maybe you should just keep your head there all the time. Then, you can't scare the shit out of me, and my pussy will be one happy girl."

He chuckled at that. "Your pussy is the greediest fucking girl I know."

"So?" I flashed a pointed look in his direction. "What are you trying to say, Thatcher?"

"That I…love her."

Yeah…that's what I thought…

"What are you looking at anyway?" His eyes moved to my laptop. "Houses? Why are you looking at houses?"

Shit.

I shrugged. "I just felt like it."

"You just felt like looking at houses?" he asked in incredulity. "The same woman who once said and I quote, *Realtors must have the most boring fucking job just looking at houses all day*."

What the fuck?
Does he all of a sudden have the memory of an elephant?
No, he doesn't. He's a man, for fuck's sake.
I mean, I could hardly get him to remember to put his dirty clothes in the laundry, but for some insane reason, his brain decided that this random piece of conversation from months and months ago would be a good thing to hold on to.

Fucking men, right?
At least we women are fair and cohesive in the way we remember shit.
We remember everything.

"I don't remember saying that," I lied. "And anyway, what are you, the fudging internet police? If I want to search houses, I'll search houses. If I want to search pictures of the blue waffle and videos of golden showers, I'll fucking do it."

"Blue waffles?" he questioned, confused.

"Not plural, just the blue waffle," I corrected. "Don't Google it unless you want to be grossed the fluff out."

"Noted," he said with a look in his eyes that told me he'd be searching the blue waffle at some point in the next few hours. "So, you're just looking at houses for fun?"

"Yep."

"Liar."

"I'm not lying."

"You're lying. And I'm honestly a little disappointed in how poorly you're doing it. Are you feeling okay, honey?"

I knew I needed to change my tactic and I needed to change it fast.

"Fine," I said in a quiet voice. "I was looking at houses for us."

"You want us to buy a house?"

"Yes," I answered, because technically, I did want us to buy a house.

"Why do you want us to buy a house? I thought you loved the apartment and living in the city?"

"I thought maybe we could use the extra space since having Ace."

"How many bedrooms do you think you'd want?"

I shrugged. "I don't know…four, I guess?"

"What about bathrooms?"

Jesus. How many questions could one man ask?

I needed to distract him before I started to lose my mind. A woman could only come up with so many lies in a fifteen-minute period.

I shut my laptop and set it on the coffee table. And without wasting a second, I took off my tank top and bra, tossing them across the living room floor. I lay back on the couch and shimmied out of my shorts and panties before discarding them on the floor, too. All the while Thatch stared down at me with a wicked gleam in his eyes.

Grabbing both breasts with my hands, I squeezed them together and pinched the nipples as I looked up at my husband and licked across my bottom lip.

"What are you doing, Crazy?"

"Playing."

"Playing?" he asked on a near growl.

"Uh-huh." I nodded. "Want to join me?"

He didn't even waste time with a response, hopping over the back of the couch and burying his face between my thighs.

Oh, hell yes…distractions are goooood…

CHAPTER 17

Wes

"Okay, okay," I called as soon as I walked into the room to a group of sex-deprived, crazy players. Apparently, my little talk at the beginning of the trip had scared them so much that they were afraid to look at women outside of the pageant proceedings either for fear those women would end up underage or affiliated in some way too. I appreciated their efforts, and if I was honest, found great enjoyment in it.

Nothing was better than making them suffer.

"I'm proud of you guys."

The group groan started in the back and traveled forward until I was being booed by over forty men.

I laughed.

"Yeah, yeah, I suck, whatever."

Quinn raised an eyebrow and sat up straighter in the front. "You're being weird."

I rolled my eyes. "I'm not. I'm being *proud*," I said, and they groaned again. "You guys took something completely out of your wheelhouse and practically stamped with fucking disaster—"

"Hey!" Georgia shouted from the back, and the players laughed.

"And handled it in a way that will actually produce positive press. Probably something along the lines of 'New York Mavericks Take Part in Miss Teen USA Pageant. No Serious Injuries Reported Despite a Close Call.'"

Raucous laughter echoed in the room as they all taunted and slapped the back of Littleton teasingly. He didn't take it lying down, though. "Whatever. Go ahead, guys. Brag like little motherfuckers about being good in a *beauty pageant*. I'm sure that'll keep your contracts signed."

Quinn sat back in his chair and added his part as always. "That's also a long-ass headline."

I shook my head and looked down to Winnie, laughing from her spot in front.

My wife.

"Dr. Winslow," I called, and she shook her head dismissively, knowing me well enough to know where this was going and hating it already.

"Come up here," I went on, only to be backed up by a chant of the entire team. "Double U, Double U, Double U."

She jumped up and stood beside me with a blush. Probably for no more reason than to quiet the near-deafening chant. "Wes—"

I knew she'd be nervous about telling the team, but there was no way in fuck I was going to work my entire career pretending she wasn't my wife. She'd always be the team physician first in the facility and have my utmost respect, but I loved her, I'd married her, and I wanted everyone to know.

"I'm happy. I want all of them to know," I explained, and within a second, her face was as soft as butter. She nodded her acceptance, and I breathed a sigh of relief.

"Want to let us in on your meeting?" Fletcher asked, and I just barely stopped myself from flipping him off. But that definitely wouldn't be professional. So I'd do it the next time I saw Kline and

Thatch, even if I didn't have a reason. Sort of like an "IOFU."

"We've got news," I announced bluntly, and a hush fell over the group, rolling from front to back like a wave.

Some of their faces dropped as they looked on and took in the tone of my voice. It was serious. At least, as serious as I could manage when a one-thousand-watt smile was making a bid to escape.

"Last night, I asked Winnie to marry me."

"Oh, shit," someone yelled in the back. "I bet she said no."

I shook my head, and Winnie talked over them. "There was no asking. You just put the ring on my finger."

"Owee!" Quinn yelled, and I laughed at his charm. God, some woman was going to be in a whole hell of a lot of trouble with him.

"And we got married this morning," I finished. For several long beats, I thought no one would say anything. But when they all got over looking at each other in shock, surprise, or for some, outright knowing, I could barely hear myself think, the crowd noise was so loud.

"Pooh's married?" Sean Phillips yelled over the hum with a boat-load of faux drama. "To you?"

Quinn jumped from his seat and ran to the front before slinging an arm around my shoulders and wrapping the other inappropriate-ly around my waist. "He's a catch!" he shouted to the delight of the now-rowdy crowd. "I'd thought we'd be together one day!" he went on.

I shoved him away and shook my head all at once as Winnie stepped under my arm to reclaim her territory.

"Hands off, Bailey."

Quinn's smile was contagious as he sank back into his seat and collected several backslaps from his closest teammates.

"Are you sure you can't do better, Dr. Double U?" Mitchell asked with a smirk and a wink. "He never smiles. I, on the other hand, have a perfectly white set of teeth I don't ever put away."

"Fake teeth," one of the other guys muttered. "He lost all of his real ones when we played Carolina."

Mitchell reached back to smack at the accuser, and it wasn't long before a slap fight broke out among the whole team. It was like a room full of way-oversized teenage girls.

"All right, all right," I yelled. "Settle down."

"'All right, all right, all right,' said Matthew McConaughey," Sean Phillips mocked.

"Everybody shut up," I said loudly, holding my smile inside until they complied.

"Marriage has already changed him," Quinn stage-whispered as happiness took over my face at the feel of my *wife's* body shaking in laughter against mine.

"Again, I'm proud of you guys. You managed to stay out of trouble this week."

"We're angels," a guy in the back offered, and I nearly choked on my laugh.

"Right. Well, if you're angels, prove it by being them tonight too. It's our last night, and there are no sanctioned activities to keep you out of trouble."

"We'll be good," Sean Phillips assured, but given who he was related to and the look on his face, it wasn't reassuring at all.

"Right." I shrugged. "If you're not, you'll be off the team."

Faces melted their humor and settled on serious—a sign it was time to move on. I let loose the smile I was holding in again.

"Now congratulate us."

Up and out of their seats, the whole room jumped into motion, their hoots and hollers surely heard all the way down the hall.

Quinn scooped Lexi out of the way of the advancing men and settled her on his shoulders as the weight of the team converged around me and her mother.

Wrapped in the arms of everything I'd created on my own, I pulled Winnie close and kissed her lips as I pictured everything we'd be able to do *together*.

CHAPTER 18

Winnie

My thigh tingled as Wes kneaded the flesh underneath my fresh-ly placed napkin, and I studied the green lean of tonight's per-fect hazel eyes. They favored blue when he wore white, black, and steely blue-grays, but tonight's light plumy purple made each green note scream. I smiled as the completely ridiculous notion that his changing eyes meant I had the next best thing to a vampire a woman could get whispered through my mind.

He certainly has the suction going for him.

"Awww, look at all of the happy couples," Dean greeted as he walked toward our table, pulling all of our moony eyes away from our significant others. At least, I assumed the others were deeply en-sconced in the depths of PDA too. They sure as hell hadn't been trying to talk to us, anyway.

All six of us were dressed up and sitting together at the fine din-ing restaurant inside Atlantis for a group dinner—without kids—to celebrate our last night in the Bahamas. A good-bye dinner of sorts.

Dean's arms were locked with two extremely tall and attractive men who seemed oddly content at just being at his side. Given the heavy starch content in his freshly pressed dress shirt and the blind devotion of his two random minions, I was starting to wonder if Dean delved into some Dom/sub kind of scenarios on the down low.

"Oh, look who it is," Georgia singsonged with a smile. "I completely forgot that you were even on this trip with us. I'm guessing you've been pretty busy with things?"

She took the words right from my mind like some kind of brain-sucking zombie. I could literally count on two fingers the number of times I'd seen Dean on this trip, and the first time was on the plane ride down.

"He looks like he's been more than busy," Cassie chimed in. "I'd say he's been stuffed full of activities since he stepped off the plane."

"Oh no, honey," Dean declared. "I do the stuffing."

"You're a top?"

Dean winked. "Something like that."

"I knew that already," Georgia gloated coquettishly, and Kline shook his head.

Cassie let out a low whistle. "Well, hot damn—"

"You want to join us for dinner tonight?" I interrupted in hopes that we'd veer the topic of discussion before it got out of hand. I could tell by the look in Cassie's eyes that she was ready to take us straight to the dirty stuff.

Dean grinned. "See? I knew you would eventually take Georgia's place as my favorite girl."

"Hey!" Georgia exclaimed. "I take offense to that."

"Good."

"You should feel really bad, you know," Georgia added. "Being mean to a pregnant lady like that. I'm in a delicate state. You should be—"

"Hold the phone." Dean held up a hand. "Pregnant?" He looked at Kline. "You fertilized her egg? Found her a roommate? Put a bun in her oven?"

"I did," Kline answered with a proud smile as the rest of us laughed. He wrapped his arm around his wife's shoulders and tucked her close to his side, pressing a soft kiss to the side of her forehead.

Dean's eyes found Georgia's, and his voice dropped to a dramatic whisper. "My little girl is all knocked up?"

Georgia's face lit up. "I am."

"Oh my God!" Dean exclaimed and quickly left his two *friends* to walk around the table and pull Georgia away from her husband and into his arms. "I'm so happy for you, sweetie," he said quietly as he hugged her tight. "So fucking happy for you. Congratulations."

Georgia's face beamed. "Thank you."

He let her go and helped her back into her seat. "When we get back to New York, we are going baby crazy. I demand it. But, fucking hell, it better be a girl. I need crimson lips and plastic kitten heels. Not goddamn hooded sweatshirts."

"Deal," she agreed as Thatch objected to even a hint of derision toward the sex of his child.

"Hey!" he contested. "Boys are just as good as girls."

Cassie put a hand to his lips and told it like it was. "Sorry, honey. He's right. Boy clothes are shit."

Dean inclined his head as if to say, "See?" I laughed deep in my throat, and Dean's eyes came back to me. "Okay, never mind, Win. Georgia is still my best girl."

My waning laugh waxed again as I waved my hand in the air. My left hand. "Whatever, diva. I see how it is."

He tilted his head to the side, eyes alert and zooming in farther and farther by the second.

Playful to high-pitched, his voice transformed in an instant. "What is that?"

"What is what?" I feigned confusion, but I pulled my hand to my chest rather than concealing it in my lap.

He put a hand to his hip and tapped a Prada toe. "That giant glittery pretty rock sitting on your left ring finger is what, Wedded Deceiver."

I held my hand in the air again and wiggled my fingers. "Oh, you mean this?"

He laughed. "Um…Fuck yes, I mean that."

"Well…" I looked at Wes and smiled, but I was no match for my husband's excitement.

"We got married," the thunder stealer remarked easily.

"Wait a minute…I was thinking fucking engaged. You're already married?"

"Yeah," Wes responded, but his eyes were still on mine.

"Jesus Christ, you heteros move motherfucking fast."

Wes chuckled and winked right at me. "The second she said yes I didn't want to give her any time to rethink her decision."

"Planning on fucking up soon?" Dean teased. "Trapping her into marriage beforehand?"

I grinned, and my husband pulled my left hand into both of his and lifted it toward his mouth to softly kiss the finger that held the symbol of our forever commitment.

"God, there is almost too much love occurring at this table right now," Dean grumbled and pretended to gag. "Hurry up, Cass. Do something crazy before this starts to go to my head. At this rate, I might wake up tomorrow morning pregnant with Elton John's baby or something."

"Pretty sure you'd need a pussy to accomplish that," Cassie retorted. "And Elton John."

"He's in the room," Dean retorted immediately.

When we all stared, he burst out laughing.

"Not really. Jesus. Look at all of you."

"He's your ultimate?"

"Um…of course, he's my ultimate," Dean responded with attitude. "Have you heard 'Tiny Dancer'? 'Your Song'? Believe me, that man is my dreamboat. He'll know it one day too."

Wes pretended to cough. "I hear Thatch gives lessons on stalking."

Thatch flipped him off.

"What about them?" Georgia asked, pointing to the two men Dean had strolled up with, who were now just waiting patiently for him outside the restaurant.

"Oh, them? They're just my fuck buddies. *Current* fuck buddies. They're working at about seventy-five percent, compared to what I'm calling the Love Boat Rendezvous," he answered without a second thought. "You don't marry those kind of men. You fuck them. You let them suck—"

Georgia held up a hand. "Yeah. Okay. We get it."

Dean smirked. "Speaking of *sucking*, I'm going to leave you guys to enjoy your last dinner in the Bahamas and your lovey-dovey bubble of marriage and babies and dreamy sighs and swoony eyes."

"And what are you going to do?" Georgia asked naïvely, and Cassie snorted in laughter.

"What do you think he's going to do, Wheorgie?"

Georgia's eyes went wide. "Oh, never mind. Keep the details to yourself and wear a condom."

"Or condoms," Cassie added kindly.

Dean pointed to her and winked. "I like where your head's at, crazy girl."

"Are you flying home with us tomorrow morning?" Kline asked, always on top of the logistics. The rest of us could be blind from pornographic exposure, and Kline would still have the awareness to make sure the actors were getting paid enough.

"Yep," Dean answered. "I'll see you guys tomorrow morning, bright and early." He moved around the table giving everyone hugs—and probably lingering a little too long with Thatch and Wes. Although, Thatch just grinned and took it all in his normal stride, wrapping his arms around Dean and hugging him so tightly his feet left the floor.

"I love you too, sweetheart," Thatch whispered. Cassie laughed and Dean swooned, popping up on his toes to put his lips to Thatch's bearded cheek.

I watched him weave through the crowd and out the door, winking and waving at other patrons as he went, even though they clearly had not one fucking clue who he was. Once he was out of sight, we gave the waitress our drink orders and relaxed into comfortable conversation about the trip and Georgia's pregnancy and the fact that Cassie thought Wes and I should have a wedding reception when we got back to New York.

"I have a feeling you want the wedding reception because of open bar and filet mignon," I said on a laugh.

"That might be part of it." Cassie grinned. "But how am I supposed to give you your gift if you don't have a wedding reception?"

Wes chuckled and held up both hands in defense of her imaginary gift. A dildo. A third for the night. Handcuffs and a ball gag. You never really knew what you were going to get when it came to Cassie Phillips-now-Kelly. "You don't need to get us anything, Cass."

His tone said, *"Seriously, don't get us anything."*

"It doesn't matter anyway," she continued. "Because my gift to you guys would be too big to bring to the reception."

"Too big?" Thatch questioned skeptically, his eyes narrowing as he wrapped his arm around the back of her chair and leaned threateningly into her. "What the fuck are we buying them? A horse?"

Unfazed, she leaned down and pulled papers from her purse and slid them across the table to Wes and me. I glanced down at the papers to find realty listings for homes in New Jersey. In Kline and Georgia's neighborhood—close to the stadium.

"What are these for?" I asked shakily, even though I already knew. I couldn't fucking believe it, but I knew.

Cassie smiled. "We've found three houses that we think the three of you—and maybe more—will be happy in. But we want you to pick the one you love the most."

"We?" Thatch chimed in. "Who's we?"

"Me and you," she answered nonchalantly. "We're giving them their dream home for their wedding present."

"What?" Thatch shouted in response. "We're buying that prick a house?"

She narrowed her eyes. "We're buying *Wes and Winnie* a house for their wedding present."

"I knew something was up when you were browsing realty listings. I fucking knew it," he muttered. "Who's paying for the house, Crazy?"

"Oh, shut up." She waved him off. "You have enough money. And it's not about the money, Thatcher. It's about the thought. And this is what friends do for each other, for fuck's sake."

"Put us down for a new family car," Kline interjected, and once again, as happened all too often, Thatch flipped him off without even looking away from his completely cracked wife.

"Pretty sure Wes and Kline didn't buy us a house when we got married," Thatch retorted. "I mean, what the fuck, honey? Have you completely lost it?"

"Oh, come on, you're a shitty friend, Thatcher," Cassie responded. "A real pain in the goddamn ass. We have to make up for that somehow."

Kline and Georgia looked at each other and at us and back to each other, and then it was all over. He started chuckling and she started giggling, and eventually, the amusement worked its way over to Wes and me, and we were doing the same.

"Cass," I said once I could catch my breath. "We love you, and we appreciate the gesture. I mean, it is so thoughtful."

"Really fucking thoughtful," Wes agreed.

"But there is no way we can let you buy us a house," I went on.

"Yeah, sweetheart," Wes added with a genuine smile. "We really can't let you do that."

"But…" Cassie started to refute, and Thatch wrapped his arm around his wife's shoulders and whispered something in her ear. She looked up at him with a devilish grin. "You promise?"

Thatch nodded.

"No bullshit?"

He shook his head and grinned.

"Well, okay, then," she said and slapped her hands down onto the table and stood. "We're going to call it a night. And we'll buy you guys a gravy boat or a Crock-Pot or something for your wedding gift. Maybe a salad spinner. You look like salad people. Sound good?"

"Wait!" Georgia protested. "You guys are leaving dinner before dinner?"

"Yep," Cassie said and slung her purse over her shoulder. "Since Melinda is watching both Lexi and Ace tonight, we're going to take full advantage of it before we head home in the morning. Who knows? Maybe we'll take a page from your and Kline's book and go full-on anal tonight."

"Cassie!" Georgia's eyes went wide, and Kline choked on a laugh—or bread. It was really one or the other. All I knew for sure was that he was motherfucking choking for real.

Thatch slapped his meaty hand on Kline's back until he coughed his way to clean air.

Georgia covered her face with both hands. "Kline, make them stop. Make them stop looking at me."

Finally safe from asphyxiation, he grinned and stood up from the table, picked his wife up out of her seat, and cradled her in his arms like a baby. She reached behind her legs to prevent a full-on Britney Spears-esque pussy shot.

"Kline!" she shrieked. "What are you doing?"

"Just saving my Benny from unwelcome anal."

Probably by taking her upstairs for the welcome kind.

"Think we should go take advantage of a free night too?" Wes whispered in my ear, and a tingle shot down my spine.

My husband, our friends. All of it was perfect. "Yes, please."

And that was that. Everyone stood up and dug in pockets and threw bills on the table in a haphazard pile.

"Is everyone really leaving dinner before actually eating dinner?

Are we a bunch of horny bastards?" Cassie asked comically, grabbing a big handful of her husband's ass as she did.

"Yep and yep," Georgia admitted as Kline set her on her feet.

Cassie squealed as Thatch started to drag her out of the restaurant, high-heeled feet fluttering to keep up, and then abruptly pulled him to a stop that made us all run right into the back of one another like a crashing train.

"Hey!"

"Jesus," Wes muttered from behind me.

"Can we at least group hug it out before we go?" Cassie asked, starting to pout.

Already nodding, I grabbed Wes's hand and pulled him closer into the huddle. "Let's hug it out, ladies," I said and held out both of my arms. Georgia, Cassie, and I hugged each other tightly. Thatch was the first to give up all pretense, wrapping his giant arms around the entire group of us, and Kline and Wes joined in before long.

All six of us stood there in the middle of the resort's fanciest restaurant in one giant group hug.

Yeah, no doubt we probably looked like a bunch of weirdos, but I had to admit it felt good. Leaning on each other, literally, there wasn't one of us who doubted we'd be able to do it forever—for whatever we needed.

"See you guys later," Kline muttered, pulling back from the group and taking Georgia with him.

"You bet your sweet ass, you will," Thatch remarked.

Wes couldn't help himself. "He actually didn't mean you. We're hoping to ditch you."

Thatch smiled wide. "Never."

Always up for the challenge of bringing it home, the last thing that was said before we officially parted ways for the night came straight from Cassie's lips. "I hope everyone in this restaurant thinks we're leaving dinner early for a gang bang."

Okay. It was the last thing until Thatch raised an eyebrow in intrigue.

"No!" we all shouted at once.

"Think about it," he pushed as we started to walk away. "*Billionaire Bad Boners: A Pornographic Trilogy.*"

I bit my lip to contain my laugh as Wes's hand settled into the small of my back.

"Shut up, Thatcher," Cassie advised.

I could hear his smile from across the room. "Okay, Crazy. I'll shut up. For now."

THE END

Loved the Billionaire Bad Boys Series and ready for more from Max Monroe?

Don't worry, there will be more. Funny, swoony, and sexy kind of more.

We have some very exciting things coming down the pipeline!

Stay up to date with us by signing up for our newsletter:

www.authormaxmonroe.com/#!contact/c1kcz

You may live to regret much, but we promise it won't be this.

Seriously. We'll make it fun. We always do, right? ;)

If you're already signed up, consider sending us a message to tell us how much you love us. We really like that. ;)

And you really don't want to miss what's next from Max Monroe.

Even though we just said goodbye to Kline, Thatch, Wes and the girls, we have plenty more heading your way. Including, but definitely not limited to, an insider's view into some of our favorite New York Mavericks.

And there's no need to be sad about saying goodbye to Big-dick and Supercock and the rest of the Billionaire Bad Boys gang; you'll be seeing lots of appearances by your favorite characters in future books.

We're certain we'll never be able to get rid of Thatch. He's like one of those bad, annoying, itchy rashes that never go away!

Preorder future Max Monroe books (when available) here: www.authormaxmonroe.com/books

CONTACT INFORMATION

Follow us online:

Website: www.authormaxmonroe.com

Facebook: www.facebook.com/authormaxmonroe

Reader Group:www.facebook.com/groups/1561640154166388

Twitter: www.twitter.com/authormaxmonroe

Instagram: www.instagram.com/authormaxmonroe

Goodreads: https://goo.gl/8VUIz2

ACKNOWLEDGEMENTS

Seeing as this is the last book in the Billionaire Bad Boys series, we're going to handle our THANK YOUS a little differently. We've never really been conventional anyway, so this shouldn't come as too much of a surprise. :)

Monroe: I can't believe the series is over.

Max: I can't believe I'll finally get to sleep without Thatch trying to commandeer my dreams.

Monroe: You have dreams about Thatch?

Thatch: You dream about me, Max?

Max: What the hell? How'd you get in here? This is the acknowledgements. The book is done. The series is over. Why. Are. You. Here?

Thatch: [raises a pointed brow] Probably because I'm like a bad, annoying, itchy rash that will never go away...

Monroe: I don't even feel bad for putting that in there. The fact that you're here, in the middle of the acknowledgements, is proof that you are in fact like a bad rash.

Max: More like an STD...

Monroe: Exactly! Like herpes. Once you get it, you have it for life.

Thatch: You're keeping me for life? Aww...you two are the sweetest.

Monroe: How do we make him go away?

Max: I have no idea.

Cassie: There's really no way to get rid of him. Trust me, I know from experience.

Monroe: [sighs] You too?

Cassie: [grins] Of course, I'm here, too.

Max: [looks at Monroe] You have dreams about Cassie, don't you?

Monroe: I wish I could say no to that question.

Max: Do you think we're currently dreaming? Like, maybe, we're not even writing the acknowledgements right now... maybe we're just dreaming about writing the acknowledgements...

Monroe: Like the inception of acknowledgment writing?

Max: Yeah. Exactly like that. Or, these characters have driven us to the point of insanity.

Monroe: [nods] It's honestly a toss up which situation is reality at this point.

Max: Do you think they serve wine in psych wards?

Monroe: I hope so.

Max: Me too.

Monroe: Do you think they serve THANK YOUs in psych wards?

Max: Probably not.

Monroe: Should we just go ahead and say our THANK YOUs now? I mean, just in case this isn't a dream and we're not in fact sitting in padded rooms…

Max: Probably a good idea.

Monroe: THANK YOU!

Max: That's it? Just one blanket 'thank you'?

Monroe: THANK YOU TO OUR READERS! YOU GUYS ARE THE BEST! YOUR LOVE AND SUPPORT MEANS THE WORLD TO US!

Max: That's better. But I honestly think you could avoid screaming it.

Monroe: [whispers] Thank you to our beautiful editor Lisa. You are the light of our life, the fire in our loins—

Max: I mean, say it loud enough for them to actually hear it. And seriously? Fire in our loins? She doesn't cause our yeast infections. She makes our books clean and pretty.

Monroe: Hey, don't judge. I might be writing this from a padded room. I'm not exactly in a sane state of mind. Anyway, we really

really love Lisa. She might as well be the fire in our loins at this point.

Max: [shakes head] Nope. Still doesn't work. I'm honestly wondering if that statement just made this the last book she'll ever edit for us.

Monroe: Sorry if I made it awkward, Lisa!

Max: How about we just try to get through these thank yous without anymore weird shit?

Cassie: Good idea.

Thatch: Personally, I was a fan of the fire in our loins.

Monroe: [sighs] Yeah, let's get through these before the acknowledgements end in Cassie offering breastfeeding services to our readers.

Max: Good idea.

Max: Thank you to our agent Amy! We need you! We love you! Don't leave us!

Monroe: Thank you to our cover designer Sommer! You are so pretty! And we love you so much!

Max: Thank you to our OGs! You ladies are amazing! We love you!

Monroe: Thank you to the CLYs! #CampLoveYourself4eva

Max: Thank you to our Counselor Feathers! We don't know what we'd do without you ladies! You. Are. The. Best!

Monroe: THANK YOU for reading. That goes for anyone who's bought a copy, read an ARC, helped us beta, edited, or found time in their busy schedule just to make sure we didn't completely fuck everything up by missing our deadline. Thank you for supporting us, for talking about our books, and for just being so unbelievably loving and supportive of our characters. You've made this our MOST favorite adventure thus far.

Max: And THANK YOU to every blogger who has read, reviewed, posted, shared, and supported us. Your enthusiasm, support, and hard work does not go unnoticed. We wish we could send you your very own Billionaire Bad Boy as thanks. We can't. We checked with UPS and they said no. Also, there's no way in hell we could find a box big enough to fit Thatch's big head in and Kline is too fucking smart to trick into something like illegal transportation of a fictional character.

Monroe: And finally, THANK YOU to the people who love us. Thank you for all of your patience and understanding and unwavering support. We couldn't do any of this without you. You make life grand and we love you so much.

Max: Is it time to go to the Bahamas?

Monroe: Hell yes!

Max: Think anyone will notice if we're gone for six months?

Cassie: Ohhh, we love the Bahamas! Can we go again, Thatch?

Thatch: I'm game, honey.

Max: Never mind.

Monroe: Yeah. Never mind. Let's just start the next book.

Max: Yes. Something completely different.

Monroe: Without any characters from the Billionaire Bad Boys Series.

Thatch & Cassie: Hey!

Max: [ignoring them] You know, I think we should revisit that one book we were talking about.

Monroe: [eyes light up] The one with the really sexy...

Max: [nods] Yep. That's the one.

Monroe: Let's do it.

Thatch: [watches Max & Monroe leave] Wait...where are you going?

Cassie: I think they just up and left us, T.

Thatch: [smirks] Yeah...that ain't happenin', Crazy. Max & Monroe are stuck with us forever.

Cassie: Forever? How the fuck are we going to manage that?

Thatch: [winks] Don't worry, honey. I've got some plans...

Made in the USA
Coppell, TX
26 July 2020

31747863R00079